*Rick took a long quivering breath before meeting Heidi's gaze. "Promise not to laugh?" he asked.*

*"Okay. All right."*

*"Well, you might think it's funny. I have to be sure."*

*"I am. How hilarious can a scholarship be?"*

*Rick squared his shoulders. "Okay. Here goes. I am competing for the Young Miss Homemaker award."*

*Heidi didn't say anthing, but Rick was positive that her lips were twitching.*

*"You promised," he said reproachfully.*

*"Who's laughing? Go on!"*

*"The award is two thousand dollars," he said doggedly.*

*"Wow! That's the biggest scholarship offered at our school!"*

*"You've got it. And it's the only chance I'll ever have to get my degree in computer programming and analysis."*

Dear Readers:

In our last letter we told you about *Journey's End*, the first of Becky Stuart's series featuring Kellogg, Carey and Kellogg's faithful dog, Theodore. In book #2, *Someone Else*, to be published in February, the famous trio solves another mystery: just where has Carey's neighbor gone? Theodore is the first to know, and you may be sure the answer is a surprise to all concerned.

Now we would like to call your attention to *Orinoco Adventure*, January book #169, Elaine Harper's first Romantic Adventure. Romantic Adventures are Blossom Valley Books that are not set in Blossom Valley. Each one will have a map so that you may follow for yourself the travels of the characters. Look for the words Romantic Adventure on the front cover, under the Blossom Valley arch. You'll be glad you did!

Nancy Jackson
Senior Editor
FIRST LOVE FROM SILHOUETTE

# THE NEW MAN
## Carrie Lewis

Published by Silhouette Books New York
**America's Publisher of Contemporary Romance**

Thanks to Bill Acton for his journalistic expertise
and also to Laura Kay...just because.

SILHOUETTE BOOKS
300 E. 42nd St., New York, N.Y. 10017

Copyright © 1986 by Carrie Lewis

Distributed by Pocket Books

All rights reserved, including the right to reproduce
this book or portions thereof in any form whatsoever.
For information address Silhouette Books,
300 E. 42nd St., New York, N.Y. 10017

ISBN: 0-373-06172-2

First Silhouette Books printing January 1986

10 9 8 7 6 5 4 3 2 1

All the characters in this book are fictitious. Any
resemblance to actual persons, living or dead, is purely
coincidental.

SILHOUETTE, FIRST LOVE FROM SILHOUETTE and colophon are
registered trademarks of the publisher.

America's Publisher of Contemporary Romance

Printed in the U.S.A.

RL 5.8, IL Age 11 and up

**First Loves from Silhouette by Carrie Lewis**

*Head in the Clouds* #100
*Call of the Wild* #110
*The New Man* #172

**CARRIE LEWIS** comes from a family of pilots, as First Love readers may have guessed from *Head in the Clouds*. Before becoming a full-time writer she held down a variety of jobs. Among them she lists guidance counselor, secretary, waitress, deli manager and salesclerk. She now lives in the Arizona desert with her husband and their two small children.

# Chapter One

It started like many of his other dreams. Billowy clouds, hazy edges and blurry people without eyes or noses. Because dreams unfold second by second, with no apparent direction and lots of last-minute changes, Rick Masterson was having trouble figuring out what was going on.

He was standing on the first step of a sleek private jet. His name was printed along the shiny stream-lined side, so he guessed the expensive plane belonged to him.

Not a bad start.

The setting was dramatic and not your run-of-the-mill bedside story backdrop, either. A huge crowd of people were gathered around him. The First Family, including six cousins and four large security guards, was crammed on the top of a nearby limo, each of them stretching to their prestigious toes to get a better look at him. Several bands were playing, lots of TV cameras were rolling closer, and a "Welcome to Washington, Rick!" blimp was hovering overhead.

This wasn't going to be any ordinary dream.

An aide handed a pair of diamond-studded binoculars to him, and he took a closer look at the mass of bodies. Eager-faced people were everywhere. They appeared to have come from all the different nations of the world. There were dignitaries, businessmen, several armies, rock singers, doctors, lawyers, dogcatchers and entire villages of sheepherders.

And girls. There was an incredible amount of pretty girls. Probably several billion of them from every country Rick guessed existed.

He immediately began to search for Joany. She was from America. Born in his own hometown to be exact. A girl that shone amongst others, like pearly smooth jade against gray gravel.

Joany could be found in nearly all his dreams. Daytime, nighttime, past, present and future, it didn't matter. She'd had a special place in his heart from the first moment he'd discovered he had one.

Just as he thought he spotted her, several Rick Masterson bodyguards ushered him down the remaining aluminum steps to a nearby stage. Instantly singing rockets arced toward the sky, and brilliant expanses of color burst with ear-blasting bangs. The master of ceremonies, a famous performer who wore a pale-yellow suit and one glittering glove, beat on the microphone to get everyone's attention.

"And now," he announced, "what you've all been waiting for! The winner of winners! The man of men! The unanimously selected recipient of the award of awards... Rick Masterson, man of the universe!"

The multitudes exploded in applause. The baby-faced guy began to dance and reached a sparkling gold trophy the size of a vacuum cleaner toward Rick. It was the figure of a boulder-armed man holding a piano above his head and had the words "Man of The Universe" inscribed on the side.

Many millions of girls fainted.

Just as he was about to seize the prize, he felt the hairy legs of a horsefly tickling his nose. He swatted at his face, and, like a whiff of apple pie on a windy day, his dream vanished.

Where was he anyway?

He opened his eyes to searing white sunlight. The horsefly wasn't a horsefly at all, but a turquoise-blue dragonfly who was now zigzagging away to find a safer station than his nose. He was floating in Rose Petal Lake, in a rented row boat, with his best friend B.R.

He sighed and leaned back again. Tomorrow was the first day of school. It was phase one of a scheme that would probably send the entire town into a head spin, ruin his reputation as a normal sort of guy, make him a social outcast and cause his own loving family to reject him.

It wasn't that Rick enjoyed doing stupid things that would most likely ruin his life. Actually he was pretty conservative. And shy. Not so much around people, but with girls. Especially with Joany.

As far as Rick was concerned, there was nothing else he could do. He had to follow through with the bizarre scheme. There was no other solution. He'd already tried. Unbelievably hard, too. Rick's problem stemmed from his acute lack of monetary assets and his inadequate station in life.

He was broke.

It was incredibly simple, yet vastly complicated. All summer he'd worked to increase his bank account. While other boys were romping around pools and vegetating on science-fiction movies, Rick had battled weeds, tamed unruly yards and scalped undisciplined trees. The palms of his hands were as tough as asphalt and still tainted green from his three-month war with plants. He'd gotten so many landscaping jobs that he'd had to buy a truck to keep up with things. It needed engine work, so that combined with maintenance, insurance and other business-related costs, it not only ate up all his profits but also consumed most of his existing savings, as well. Everything would have been all right if the summer had only lasted six more months, enough time to get his initial investments back. But Rick couldn't reset the calendar, and fall was snarling at his heels before he'd ever gotten the chance to recover. There wasn't much time to earn the money he needed to go to college now. The crazy scheme was the one hope he had.

## The New Man

He moaned aloud at the surety of the fact.

"A sea monster!" Startled by the unexpected sound, B.R., a lanky boy with the physique of a chopstick, sat erect sending scores of sporadic ripples to reflect slivers of sun from the lake's dark surface. His eyes narrowed cautiously. "I heard a sea monster."

"It was only me," Rick reassured him. "I was thinking about phase one of the plan."

B.R.'s bony elbows clunked against the wood as he fell back to his makeshift bed. "Phew. That was close. I happen to believe every word that's ever been written about Loch Ness."

"We're thousands of miles from where the Loch Ness Monster is supposed to live."

"Migration, my friend. If birds migrate, then what makes you think that monsters don't?"

"Ya know, B.R., sometimes you sound like you're visiting from La La Land." Rick screwed his finger into his head.

"I have a discerning mind."

"You're a coward."

"Careful."

"There's nothing wrong with this lake."

"Oh, yeah? Then how come we're the only ones out here?"

"Listen, I'm taking another swim before we have to get the boat back. Do you want to come?"

B.R.—Bones and Ribs—shaded his eyes to peer across the ominously silent depths. "I'll let you test the waters first. If you're still floating in five minutes, I'll join you. No need in both of us becoming lunch."

In some aspects of life, B.R. was truly the epitome of the word fear. In others, he could almost be considered brave.

Take women, for example. Where Rick was overly quiet around females, B.R. could make conversation with any girl in school who was willing, regardless of her social status or any overwhelming physical attributes she might possess. No matter how popular or attractive she was, he never became nervous or said things that would qualify him for the World's Almanac of Retarded Remarks to the Opposite Sex.

That wasn't so easy for most guys.

His other fine points included a high IQ and a dry wit.

This combination of traits, though, brought him as much trouble as it did laughs. He was forever getting himself stuck in his own patch of hilarious quicksand... which is why Rick had befriended him over ten years ago.

Rick had discovered B.R. hooked backward by his belt to a chain link fence. At the all-knowing age of seven, B.R. had tried to counsel a twelve-year-old on his mathematics. As tactful then as he was today, he'd told the boy—who was triple his size, easy—that his brain could fit in the skull of a tuna fish. Maybe even a clam. Because of this lack of diplomacy, he was always being stuffed into things. In second grade, it had been a waste basket. In third, a trash can. And in fourth, the closet in the principal's office.

Life had become easier for B.R. only because Rick had stayed at his side throughout their school years.

Rick was undoubtedly a great friend to have. Loyal, caring and honest. He may have been reserved around girls, but he held the respect and favor of the boys, and most of the kids knew who he was.

Rick dove off the boat. His muscular body sliced through the murky water and disappeared below. For some, diving in and out of a small rowboat without eventually capsizing it, would've been an impossibility. Rick made it look simple, as though he were bailing in and out of an easy chair.

His blond hair bobbed into sight a full minute later, a few yards from where he'd jumped in. He swam back with quick easy strokes, as graceful as a dolphin. He hung his arms over the side of the boat, tilting the whole thing dangerously close to the surface.

B.R. clung nervously to an oar. "Isn't there a log or a duck, or a barbell somewhere you can hold onto instead of my ship?"

Rick ignored him. "Are you sure there's absolutely no other way to make this plan work except for me to take home economics?" he questioned.

"Positive. There's no out-of-towners coming to Redona offering any athletic scholarships, and Sally Bell will beat you out of any academic ones. It won't do you any good to hash over it again. There's only one group that's sponsoring a scholarship you can still qualify for at this late date."

"The Redona Society of American Homemakers," Rick began, banging his head against the side of the boat.

B.R. shrugged. "Who would've thought a local club of women could make such a generous offer?"

"Two thousand dollars. That's a lot of bake sales," Rick said.

"And brassieres."

"Bazaars."

"Do you really feel it's necessary to hang on the side of the boat?"

Rick began to rock it mischievously, but it was B.R. who, in his panic to steady things, leaned too much to the side, sank into the depths and emerged again dog-paddling.

Laughing, Rick floated backward to enjoy their last remaining minutes under the warm sun. In his estimation, the past summer of backbreaking side jobs would be "easy pie" compared to some of the feats he would need to perform to win the scholarship. The Redona Society of American Homemakers was not offering its award without some stiff prerequisites; rules that would discourage any sensible-minded boy.

A. You had to look like a good homemaker with good homemaking qualities. That simple statement entailed all the complexities of cooking, sewing, good grooming and social consciousness.

B. You had to like children and exhibit healthy *mothering* qualities.

C. You needed to have a high academic record so the club could be assured that you would do well in your chosen field in college.

The only thing Rick was obviously qualified for was the good-grades part. Since the club had put the word "Miss" into the title of their award, there was a strong probability that they weren't expecting any males to apply. Still, they had made a public announcement to the town that the sex of their applicants wouldn't affect the final judging.

A big mistake on their part.

Rick didn't like the idea of rejection or embarrassment. It was a simple matter of what was and wasn't. What could be and couldn't. Rick was intelligent, but he wasn't rich. He could be a computer analyst, but he couldn't get his degree with such a pitiful bank account. His only remaining option was to try for the Young Miss Homemaker Scholarship.

He'd thought it out very carefully, and with B.R.'s help, he'd reasoned that there was a chance he could win the award. It would take hard work, self-discipline, dedication and insanity. But the two friends had laid out a game plan that actually made the crazy idea possible. Of course, he wasn't thrilled with the thought.

He'd already suffered through one horrible nightmare because of it. It was the exact opposite of the dream he'd had earlier in the boat. His name had been called in front of a huge auditorium of people. He was asked to walk on stage and accept an award, just like before.

But this time, as soon as his foot hit the first step to the platform, a high heel appeared on the back of his tennis shoe. As he continued up the stairway, a flowered hat popped on his head. When he'd reached the podium, he'd also acquired a pair of pastel knee-highs, a ruffled apron and a purse. He reached his hands outward, expecting to receive the two-thousand-dollar prize, and the announcer, Joany, who was dressed in tuxedo and tie, placed a bottle of perfumed hand lotion in his palm instead.

He'd woken up in a cold sweat. It took several long wheezing seconds to realize it had all been his imagination, that it was only a nightmare. Logically, if he applied himself to winning the Young Miss Homemaker Scholarship, he really, seriously, wouldn't need to sacrifice his masculinity.

Would he? The first day of school tomorrow would also be his first test.

Second period. Home economics.

It was the best place to begin learning about becoming a homemaker. He sincerely doubted that there would be any other males joining him in class, except maybe Rex D'Antonio, alias Wolf, who wouldn't be enrolling in an all-girl class just to learn to crack eggs.

Wolf wasn't one of Rick's favorite acquaintances. He had too slick of a look about him. Slippery hair, sleazy remarks and a slithery personality. He had a vengeful attitude, too, and always held grudges against anyone who angered him, often releasing the air from the offender's car tires to retaliate. Wolf was also one of the boys responsible for stuffing B.R. in the heavy-duty Glad bag in third grade. A true creep from the moment he learned to walk!

"Okay," B.R. panted. "It's been wonderful getting all wet and mossy. Now how do you climb back into this thing?"

"Let me get in first, and I'll help balance it." In one swift movement Rick was inside the boat and stretching his taunt arm toward B.R.

B.R. felt himself being lifted upward as though he weighed no more than a minnow. "You sure don't look the type to be wearing an apron."

"Thanks."

"Unless, of course, it was green. You know, with those cute little ruffles you sometimes see on girls. And those big bows that tie—hey!"

A spray of water shot skyward as Rick released his hold, sending B.R. bottom first into the lake again. He bobbed back up spitting and sputtering and wiping his eyes. "I can tell you're going to be very touchy about things this year," he coughed. "Not to worry. If you can't count on your best friend not to tease you, who can you trust?"

Rick's eyes narrowed. "Only my mother, no doubt."

"A dozen eggs?" Mrs. Masterson raised an eyebrow and popped two slices of bread in Rick's hand as she brushed past him to the refrigerator. "What in the world do you need to take twelve eggs to school for?"

That's my mom for you, Rick thought to himself. Never questions. Always trusts. He slid the two pieces of bread into the toaster and cranked the nob.

"B.R. thought I would probably be needing them for a class project."

"But it's just the first day."

"I want to get a good grade."

"I guess so." She sloshed orange juice into three glasses and set them on the table in a rush. "You're not going to throw them at anyone, are you?"

"Call me naive, Mom, but I don't think that would help me get an *A*."

"Maybe a grade AA?" Mrs. Masterson broke into self-amused chuckles and reached up several feet to ruffle her hand in her son's curls. "I know!" she said suddenly. "You're still thinking of taking that cooking course, aren't you?"

"Home economics." Rick was going to explain why, but he lost his train of thought when he detected the smell of smoke.

Maybe it was the school. The home-economics room?

Mrs. Masterson covered her mouth as if to keep from laughing.

"Please don't feel you should act with sensitivity on my account," Rick commented dryly.

"I'm sorry, dear. It's just that I can't imagine you standing in front of a stove. I mean, you can't even make toast without charring it."

Toast! Rick swung around and slapped the antique machine with the palm of his hand. It released its hostages dry, black and smoldering, shooting them toward the ceiling for all his critics to see.

"I'm going to have to scrape them. Your father won't eat bread if it looks too much like flattened briquettes."

"Sorry, Mom. I forget that this old thing doesn't pop up by itself."

"You know what broil is?"

"Sure. It's related to boil. It's what you do to steaks and cakes."

"Well, you got half of it right."

"By the end of the semester, I'll be able to master almost any cuisine. Baked Alaska, soufflé. Maybe even toast." He leaned down to kiss her on the cheek. "I've gotta go, though. B.R. and I are carpooling."

"Will you get something to eat at school?"

"Sure. I'll make myself an omelet." He grabbed the carton of eggs and darted out the door.

"Don't forget to cook them first!" she called after him.

Eggs. Who knew they could be so much trouble? They nearly slid off the car seat every time Rick stopped at an intersection. He couldn't turn the box in any convenient way while he carried them for fear they'd bump into each other and crack. No tripping, no running and no colliding with any bodies in the crowded hall. Of course, there were all the remarks from the kids, too. "Make some new friends over the summer, Rick?" "Looking for a nest?" "Hungry?"

And when he'd finally gotten the fragile white objects to his second-period class, was he rewarded with praise or glory?

Not at all. The dour home-economics instructor, Mrs. Bristol, eyed him doubtfully. She didn't trust males in her class; that was apparent immediately. Wolf D'Antonio didn't help matters any by grinning and nodding at all the girls as they filed in. His motives were as obvious and greasy as his hair. Rick resented the fact that Wolf was ruining his own chances for a good first impression. Mrs. Bristol's lips were growing more and more puckered with each succeeding leer he gave his new feminine classmates.

Realizing that he would never get a favorable response from his instructor, he finally turned his attention to the room's entrance, too. But, when he saw Joany Rhoads walk in, he hastily switched his gaze forward again.

How could he have been so dumb! He'd never thought to check the roster to see if she would be taking the course at the same period he was! If he'd known, he would've switched the time. Changed schools, or cities, or something.

He slunk down in his chair wondering how the girl of his dreams was going to react when she saw him sitting in her home-ec class with a carton of eggs under his nose.

What a way to meet again after three long months!

He watched her stroll through the room and take a seat two rows down from him.

Dark-haired, brown-eyed Joany Rhoads. She had a slim, athletic figure that could even make a boy forget his sagging bank account. She had an air of confidence about her, more so than any of the other girls Rick knew. And she was pretty. Gorgeous, as a matter of fact.

"Rick!" she exclaimed, leaning forward so she could see him better. "What are you doing here?"

"It's a long story," he replied, trying to cover over any signs of hyperventilation. "How was your summer?"

"Pretty good. I was hoping you'd stop over and go swimming sometime."

"I've been busy. Lots of yard jobs and stuff."

The conversation stopped there, a dead-end alley. Rick just wasn't good at idle talk, especially when his heart was whizzing crazily in his chest, like a runaway balloon.

The bell rang. Mrs. Bristol gazed over the room, a general inspecting recruits. She gave a short, tight smile before she began to explain her schedule for the following two weeks, what the class would learn and what she expected from them in return.

Rick listened intently. He tried to ignore the fact that he was the only person in the room with eggs in front of him. Later he would mutilate B.R. for it.

People with such a bent sense of humor didn't deserve to live past seventeen anyway.

"Now everyone will need a partner for the semester. I've decided to let you girls, er, you people, select your own this year," Mrs. Bristol continued.

"We'll need to share heating units, appliances and the ovens."

Several pairs of eyes wandered toward Rick, tall, sinewy and always friendly. At the same time, Wolf's gaze surveyed the large female population surrounding him.

Mrs. Bristol's sixth-sense radar picked up on the unnecessary eye contact like a two-inch magnet to a ton of metal. Within the same few seconds she quickly added, "Except for the boys in the class. They would probably do better working with each other."

Joany Rhoads leaned forward and gave Rick a helpless shrug. A sudden warm feeling glowed inside him. She'd actually hoped that they could be partners! Pals.

Mates!

Well, maybe not mates... but definitely the two of them sharing the same oven, side by side, for one entire semester.

While everyone busied themselves looking for and selecting colleagues, Wolf changed places with the girl sitting beside Rick and moved his books to the adjoining desk.

"Hey, Rick, what's happening? Rob a chicken coop on the way to school?" he chaffed.

"I thought we'd need these today. B.R. suggested it."

"B.R.?" He smirked.

"Yeah. Great sense of humor that guy."

Wolf glanced around the room. "This is a supreme bummer." He sighed, a gloomy expression beneath his oiled hair.

"What?"

"All these wild women around me, and I'm here with you. I didn't take this bean-eating course to learn how to pat hamburgers, you know."

"I did."

"Oh, right. And I'm the Duke of Windsor." He paused and massaged his chin thoughtfully. "Take little Joany-Oany over there. I had my sights set on her from the minute she walked into the room. Now *she's* real hamburger."

"You have a great way with words, Wolf."

"Me and her could do some fine baking together," he continued.

"Fantasy Land belongs to Walt Disney."

"Naw. She's as good as gone. When Wolf fixes his eyes on his prey, he gets it. By the end of the semester that girl won't be able to think about anyone but me." He smoothed his hair back at his temples. "She'll be overwhelmed."

Rick bristled at the thought of someone like Wolf coming within even two blocks of Joany. Rick suspected that Joany was too intelligent to fall for any scheme Wolf might try to pull, yet at the same time, she was so trusting and naive about people, he couldn't help worrying that Wolf might be able to sleaze his way into her affection.

Another worry. Rick needed to add to his collection the way he needed to fill his socks with thorns.

## Chapter Two

From the first second Rick picked up the mixer, he knew he was in deep trouble. He could imagine his hand slipping between the two silver beaters. First it would crush his fingers into liquid, then it would suck in his whole arm, twisting it around and around until it formed soft peaks.

That's what his instructions were. To put six egg whites into a chilled bowl and beat them—not with a stick—until they formed soft peaks and made meringue.

Grimly, he held a knife above his egg, ready to chop it in two and dissect the yellow part from the clear part, when Mrs. Bristol called for everyone's attention. To his relief, she demonstrated how it should be done, cracking the egg gently for an even break and then juggling the yolk in the shell halves until all the whites fell free into one of the two bowls below.

Easy. Clean. She did two more, slowly, and then finished the remaining three, cracking the shells with one hand and separating the yolks in two or three swift tosses.

Rick had been dreading the moment he would need to begin an actual food-preparation process. The first four days had been nice. They'd read from books, familiarized themselves with the equipment and had collected supplies. But now it was the end of the week. Time to separate the women from the boys.

A few moths were fluttering around in his stomach, and his fingers felt like clumsy iron clamps as he grabbed the first egg. Funny, he'd watched his mom do it a hundred times in the past, and yet he'd never cracked an egg himself. Not any that he could remember. He raised it up, and underestimating his strength, he brought it down to crunch against the edge of the bowl.

"Scoop it up," Wolf whispered, turning his body to hide the gooey accident from Mrs. Bristol. "Pick the yellow part up with your hand and then shove the rest of it over the counter in the bowl."

Rick cringed at the cool slippery texture of the yoke. It slid around as he tried to get a hold without breaking it. At last it was in his hand, and with a shudder, he flipped it into the cup. Wolf held the bowl up to counter's edge, and Rick herded the whites to slosh inside.

The second egg wasn't much better than the first. Rick was so afraid he'd smash it again that he tapped it so lightly, it barely cracked. When he tried to pull it apart, his thumb bulldozed through the side. He managed to get the yolk separated, but not without a few large sections of shell shattered amongst the whites.

By the time he got the third in, the hum of mixers had begun to vibrate around the room. Rick mopped at his forehead with the back of his arm, being careful not to get any sticky egg remains in his eyebrows. "Your turn," he told Wolf tensely.

"Me? I'm not going to do that. It's girls' work."

"What do you call me?"

"Confused."

"Here you go." Rick tapped the remaining eggs. "Three for me. Three for you."

"I'm not taking this class to impress anyone."

"But you're still in it."

"I don't even know what 'terrang' is."

"Meringue." Rick shoved the bowl at him. "Come on. You're wasting time. We're already behind."

Wolf pushed it back again. "That's right. Now ask me if I care."

The bowl returned. "You better hurry. Here comes Mrs. Bristol."

Wolf slid it back. "I'm not the one who's busting my gut for grades around here. You are."

Rick quickly picked up the fourth egg and cracked it. Wolf had a point. He wasn't concerned over what mark he would end up with at the end of the semester. If Rick waited for him to show integrity, the eggs would be laying eggs. He fumbled frantically to get the yoke separated.

Mrs. Bristol strolled closer. He could feel her black beady eyes zeroing in on his ineptness. She was only pretending to be interested in the other students. Her real intentions were to catch him in a mess, mark him as a fraud and advise all her friends in the Redona Society of American Homemakers of his failure.

He smashed the fifth and frantically tried to salvage a small amount of the white part. The sixth decided to roll around on the countertop like a lopsided marble. Just as it fell over the edge in a suicidal nosedive to the floor, Wolf caught it. Mrs. Bristol was only a few steps away.

"Crack it before she gets here!" Rick ordered.

"There isn't time!"

Wolf tossed the egg into the bowl, whole.

Rick switched on the mixer. He almost lost control of it as it chomped into the shells. A six-cylinder, sixty-mile-an-hour machine. It probably mowed lawns on weekends. He was sure it could puree a mailbox if it needed to.

Thankfully the whites were frothy enough to hide most of the egg shells by the time Mrs. Bristol peered into the mixture.

"It's not a drill, Mr. Masterson!" she exclaimed. "Do you want to scrape all the finish from the bottom of the bowl?"

"No, ma'am." Rick immediately loosened his strangulation hold on the handle and started to lift it out. Spatters of egg whites began shooting through the air, when, suddenly, he felt someone's fingers pressing gently on his arm. He followed their soft guide and lowered the beaters back into the mixture.

"We don't know whether it's time to add the crème of tartar yet, Mrs. Bristol." Joany smiled at everyone, an apology for interrupting, and discreetly removed her hand from Rick's arm. "Could you check and see, please?"

Mrs. Bristol's eyes grew smaller, blacker, meaner. "Yes, all right. I'll be back to taste this, boys," she warned as she followed Joany to her counter.

Wolf whistled beneath his breath. "She saved your ham hocks."

"Probably."

"No probably about it. Check out your shirt. Does that look like a snowstorm hit it, or what?"

Rick glanced down. Mucus all over his clothes.

"If you'd raised that cement mixer any higher, you would've covered Mrs. Bristol with terrang, too."

"Meringue."

"You were almost a memory."

Rick began to wipe at the rapidly evaporating foam on his shirt as he watched Joany and Mrs. Bristol studying the contents of a bowl. She would never cease to impress him. Now he could also add "heroics" to her long list of other qualities.

She must've felt his look on her. Suddenly she glanced up, and her soft brown eyes caught him watching her. A broad grin spread across his tanned face, a natural response to someone so beautiful and thoughtful. He switched the mixer off and mouthed the words "thank you."

She gave a slight nod and whispered, "Be more careful."

Mrs. Bristol turned around and their gazes instantly switched back to their bowls.

There wasn't enough time before the end of the period for Mrs. Bristol to taste their meringue as she had threatened to do, which meant that Rick's career as a Young Miss Homemaker candidate could be extended to at least one more class.

Wolf tried a bite, and he had to chew his way through it. The crunch of eggshells sounded from his jaws like footsteps on gravel. He quickly excused himself and darted for the rest room.

The good bowls of meringue, including Joany's, were rapidly consumed. Rick had figured that would be the best part of taking home economics. He wouldn't need to spend all his money on Alpo-for-dinner cafeteria food and could eat his own creations instead, saving cash for his college fund.

Unfortunately he wasn't counting on his cooking to be so bad.

"Aren't you going to eat your meringue?" Mary, a slender blonde, one desk over inquired.

"It's too good to touch."

She giggled.

"Can I have a taste?" Joany asked, joining them.

"Uhhhh..." Rick stalled.

"Oh, come on. It looks great."

"Looks can be deceiving."

"I'll only take a little."

"How about a bite of whatever we make next week? I promised to dedicate my first creation to B.R."

Joany pouted. "But B.R. never gives concrete opinions."

"I bet he will this time."

"Why are you taking this class anyway?"

Rick toyed with the idea of actually explaining his scheme to Joany. He might've gone through with it, too, but the bell rang and Mrs. Bristol barked that all the counters weren't cleaned off yet. Since his piece of Formica was the only space with anything still left on it, he had the distinct feeling she was addressing him. He hastily excused himself from the conversation and hurried to put his things away.

"Don't do me any favors!" B.R. coughed, pushing the container of meringue back at Rick. "What is this anyway?"

"Pie covering. It used to be all smooth, but I guess that if you don't cook it, it returns to it's original state. That runny stuff you just drank from the bottom was egg whites."

"Eggs? Raw eggs?" B.R. spat wildly at the ground.

"Eggs are good for you. They've a lot of protein."

"Is this what I have to look forward to all semester?" he sputtered, his long thin neck popping with veins. "Suffering with sandy protein?"

"Now that isn't a very encouraging thing to say. You should be building me up with praise and telling me I'll do better next time."

"Mom taught me not to fib." B.R. sucked the skin of his cheeks in so that his already thin face became a line with eyes. He released them again and exhaled. "I don't know, Rick. Maybe this whole plan of you becoming the next Young Miss Homemaker is too crazy. Maybe we stepped too far out of our league this time."

"Those were my words exactly. Remember? But you said I'd have no problem. You said it would be easy." It had all been B.R.'s idea to begin with. And if B.R. decided to change his opinion of Rick's capabilities now, he would strangle him. Turn a mixer on high until he formed soft peaks.

"Yes. I vaguely recall that." B.R.'s Adam's apple bobbed up and down as he swallowed nervously. "And thinking it over, I still say you can get the scholarship. Cooking is probably your weak point. You'll undoubtedly do much better at the child-rearing part of being a homemaker."

"Child-rearing part?"

"Yeah. Working with kids. Humpty Dump-All Nursery School. You start your volunteer work in about fifteen minutes. Did you forget?"

Rick slapped his forehead with the palm of his hand. "I sure did forget!" He pushed his pile of books and Tupperware container of meringue into B.R.'s stomach as though he were passing a football. "Can you drop these home for me? I gotta run! You'll have to catch a ride with someone else. It looks like I'm going to be late enough as it is." He started at a fast lope toward the parking lot, leaving B.R. standing in front of the high school.

"Keep your cool!" B.R. coached after him. "Think like a mother!"

Rick felt the color of crimson crawl up his neck. He glanced around to see if anyone had heard the embarrassing instructions.

Only about sixty people.

"Okay. I'll think like your *bro*-ther!" he yelled back, trying to disguise the remark. He really needed to talk to B.R. about being discreet. He didn't want anyone to get the wrong idea. It was already difficult enough trying to maintain his image while everybody saw him walk into the home-economics room each morning, without having to worry about his best friend always telling him to think like a mother as well.

A father. That's how he was trying to see himself. Like a father. In fact, applying as a volunteer aid at the Humpty Dump-All Nursery School had been much easier for him to do than registering for home economics.

Men had a lot to do with kids these days. There were uncles, brothers, fathers and grandfathers. Coaches, counselors and teachers. If you looked at it in the right light, there wasn't a thing wrong with a guy volunteering his time to work with children.

Besides, it was only for three hours on Fridays. B.R. said the judges for the Young Miss Homemaker Scholarship wouldn't see the amount of time so much as the word "volunteer." He thought they would be highly impressed with a person who donated his Friday afternoons to aid an overcrowded nursery school without any thought of pay.

The nursery school was a large pitch-roofed house that had been remodeled. It was painted bright red with pink trim, and it had a short picket fence surrounding the colorful flower beds that had been dug beneath every shutter-covered window. The words Humpty Dump-All Nursery School were printed in big childish lettering over the door, and the mailbox in front of the school was made to look like a miniature cottage.

Rick decided that any place this fun in appearance would have to be interesting to work at.

When he opened the barn-type door, confusing mixtures of smells enveloped him. Clay, coffee and Spaghetti-O's? Crayon pictures decorated the walls. Toys ranging from building blocks to three-wheel fire engines and headless dolls cluttered the faded carpet. There were the dingy traces of fingerprints on all smooth surfaces, and a half-eaten peanut-butter sandwich was stuffed in the corner of the entryway.

"Excuse me," he called above the commotion. "Is there a grown-up here?"

Suddenly a runaway tricycle burst from one of the rooms down the hall. Rick jumped out of the way just as the driver, with head bent low and a determined expression on his face, "varoomed" past him. He ducked into the doorway of its launch, and was almost hit by a flying purple penguin. Judging by the sound it made when it splatted against the wall, the bird had just gone swimming.

Probably in one of the toilets.

The room was at war. Rick couldn't tell who was fighting whom exactly, but casualties began to mount. A cute little redheaded girl with pigtails was sitting in the middle of the chaos, wailing that someone had taken her dolly hostage. A blond boy with a sprinkle of freckles across his nose stood to the side, jumping up and down and shouting for his mommy.

"Help!"

Rick thought the call sounded a bit more mature than the others and searched through the debris for someone over five.

"I'm here! In the bathroom!" The voice called again. A girl's face peaked around the corner.

Rick started across the battlefield toward her, being careful not to step on any midget soldiers. The girl appeared to be about the same age as Rick, if not younger. She was attractive with olive-toned skin and big hazel eyes. Wisps of honey-colored hair fell over her face, strands that had pulled loose from her French braid.

"Clara is ill today, and there's no one to cover for her," she explained hurriedly as she fumbled to pull the pants over the chubby bottom of a sour-faced boy. "While I was in the bathroom helping Chaddy, Beany started making the other kids crazy. He does that all the time, you know." She gritted her teeth as she glanced around the corner to spot Beany and then looked back at Rick.

"You're the volunteer, aren't you?"

"Yes."

"I'm really glad you showed up. Sometimes volunteers can be extremely flaky. No offense."

"What can I do?"

"Find Beany and stop him from further destruction."

"Which one is he?"

"The kid in the green-striped shirt. Over there. Pinning the little redheaded girl down with his knee."

"He's kind of mean, isn't he?"

"Vicious."

Rick nodded. "I'll take care of it."

Like a dogged police inspector he tromped through the litter to the curly-haired boy. "Okay, buster," he commanded. "Get off her."

Beany screwed up his face and moved to sit more squarely on his flailing victim.

"I'm going to give you one more chance before I swat your bottom." Rick gave his best Indiana Jones scowl, but the youngster wasn't impressed. In a rebellious gesture, a mocking challenge to Rick, he hit the smaller girl in the head.

Her cries became tearful.

A flush of anger reddened Rick's face. "All right! That's it!" In one swift sweeping motion he had Beany dangling helplessly over his arm, his rear turned upward for an easier target.

Except for a few sobs the room fell silent as he raised his hand ominously in the air.

Ready... aim...

"Stop!" The pretty girl sat Chaddy on the floor and ran over, frantically waving her arms. "You can't spank him!"

Beany twisted around to stick his pink, pointed tongue at Rick. "Nanny, nanny, poo-poo, nanny, nanny, poo-poo!" he chanted.

"What do you mean I can't spank him? What am I supposed to do with him?"

"He has to stand in the corner for five minutes."

"Why can't I hit him?"

"It's a rule. No spanking."

"The guy deserves it."

"I know. But we can't. We could be liable. Here—" she took Beany from Rick's arms and plopped him on the floor "—watch what I do."

"Don't squeeze my arm! If you squeeze my arm, I'm telling my brother. He'll beat you up. Pulverize you!" Beany yelled.

The young woman gave Rick a twisted sort of smile and then hooked her fingers on to Beany's arm.

"Ow! Let go!"

She dragged him by the arm to the corner. "Five minutes. If you move once, it's six, or seven. Got it, Mr. D'Antonio?"

His bottom lip quivered.

She brushed her hands together triumphantly and turned to their openmouthed audience. "Okay. The rest of you guys pick up this mess. As soon as the floor is clean, we'll have snacks, and I'll introduce you to our new friend."

## The New Man

The little red-haired girl quieted her crying and wiped the tears from her cheeks. She hooked her hand around Rick's finger and stared up at him. "Fank you, mistur."

"You're welcome. What's your name?"

"Sowah."

"Sandra?"

"No. Sowahh. Sooowahhhh," she said, trying to sound it out.

Rick grinned down at her. "That's a nice name."

She tucked her chin to her chest shyly and began rocking back and forth.

"Sarah, are you okay?" the girl asked, glancing at Rick. "It's her first day. Her parents are new in town," she explained.

"Wes, mam."

"Good. Now go help the others. Hurry up. We're going to have oatmeal cookies and milk." She patted Sarah's back, then took her hand to lead her to join the rest of the kids in the massive cleanup, then reached toward Rick. "My name is Heidi," she said, blowing at her wisps of hair.

"Rick." He took her hand and shook it. "So that's the best we can do around here? Seven minutes in a corner?"

She laughed. "That's it. It's old-fashioned, but it seems to work. You don't need to do it to most kids, though. Only Beany. He's older than the rest and a supreme bully."

"You called him Mr. D'Antonio. Is that his real last name?"

"Yes. Do you know the family?"

"Sure do. I got déjà vu just watching him. He's almost a spitting image of his older brother—personality-wise. We go to school together."

"Tell me then, will Beany ever change?"

"It gets a little better. He'll stop sitting on girls and start chasing them instead. To give you an idea of what I'm talking about, his brother is nicknamed Wolf."

"I'm not surprised."

Rick decided she had all the right instincts. He also knew that if he'd seen her in school before, he would've remembered her. "Do you go to high school in town?" he asked.

"No. I'm from Ridgemont."

"Then how did you get here so fast? I was almost late, and I really hustled!"

She laughed and brushed at her flagging whisps of hair. "I didn't just come a few minutes ago. My last class is over at ten forty-five, and I start work here at noon. That's plenty of time to get something to eat and drive to Redona."

"You're that far ahead in your required credits?"

"I really took on a heavy class load my freshman and sophomore years."

"I guess so." Rick grinned. "You make me feel lazy."

She flashed a pleasant smile. "Don't be too impressed. My parents had a lot to do with it. They're both teachers. Come on. I'll show you how we pass out the snacks."

## The New Man

Rick followed her to a half-size refrigerator positioned safely behind Clara's desk. As he walked he felt all eyes on him.

"These kids are pretty nosy, aren't they?"

Heidi glanced over her shoulder. "They're not used to seeing a young man in here. You're the first male who's ever worked at Humpty Dump-All."

"Really?"

"I think it's a great idea. The kids need a male role model."

Rick felt a tugging at his pants leg and looked down at the small blond boy with the sprinkle of freckles across his nose.

"Yes?" Rick bent over so they could look directly in each other's faces. "What can I do for you, sport?"

The boy broke into a shy smile.

"Wou, wou, would you be my mommy?" he asked.

*So much for the male role model.*

## Chapter Three

So you want to work in the mines all your life? Fine. That's what's going to happen if you drop out of home economics." B.R. was arguing so intensely, even the veins in his ears were bulging. He was keeping in step with Rick down the long sidewalk that connected the school with the parking lot. Their strides were quick, long and in precise time with one another. "You'll end up just like your dad. Busting your back all your life at the same job and still barely being able to scrape up enough money to make a living."

"You make it sound as though we're ready for the food lines," Rick objected, switching his books to his other hand. "Dad did fine. He's got a house, a truck and a trailer, all free and clear. He also has some money tucked away to retire on. He may not be able to travel around the world every summer, but he can go fishing anytime he wants."

"Okay. So you'd be satisfied with the money. But what about your brain? Do you want to use your back all your life, or do you want to apply your mind at least a few times a week?"

Rick was conscious of the taut muscles that formed his broad shoulders. He'd developed most of them through long hours of manual labor. Like his father, he was a steadfast worker. He would never admit it to anyone, but he often enjoyed a grueling day of physical labor. He always felt so relaxed and carefree afterward, as though he'd completed what was expected of him, and now deserved to enjoy himself. Whenever he sat around too long with nothing to do, he became anxious inside. Bored and uneasy.

Yet, he knew he wouldn't be happy being a miner.

He loved the complex challenges of mastering computers. He liked programming them and explaining their intricate functions to others. His brain buzzed with information, input and output, problems, puzzles and solutions whenever he sat down in front of the only screen in the world that talked back to human beings.

As much as he enjoyed giving his body a good healthy workout, he treasured putting his mind through a stiff grind more. He would make a great computer programmer, but only a mildly contented miner.

"This conversation is old," he said. "Sure I want to use my head more than I want to use my brawn. But as you so tactfully brought up I don't have a rich dad the way you do. There's no college fund sitting around in my name."

"Violins and tears." B.R. mocked a sniff. "You have the same chance as anyone for winning the Young Miss Homemaker Scholarship."

"Correct me if I'm wrong, but don't female homemakers outnumber male homemakers about fifty million to one?"

"I think those figures are a bit outdated."

"I'd say it's close enough."

"I think you're turning chicken."

"I'm being reasonable."

"Cluck, cluck, cluck."

Rick snorted. "Do you have any idea what I did last week?"

"You made a bad batch of gritty Styrofoam and played ring-around-the-rosy with some kids."

"Does that sound easy to you?"

"Sure. People do it all the time."

"No, B.R.," Rick snapped. "*Women* do it all the time. Do you want to know what happened to me at the nursery school?"

"I guess I can take it."

"A little boy came up to me and asked if I would be his mommy. That's what happened. His mommy!" He stomped past B.R. toward the school. "How much is a guy supposed to take?"

"Ah, come on, Rick," B.R. argued, starting after him. "You can't be so touchy about things. It was a two-year-old kid who didn't know any better."

"All the same, I don't think I'm going to be able to go through with this." In his frustration, Rick accidentally bumped into another boy, sending him sprawling off the sidewalk. "Sorry, buddy," he quickly apologized. "And I'm dropping out of home economics, too."

"Cluck, cluck, cluck."

He ignored B.R., determined not to give in. He had as much pride as anyone else. There was more to the word macho than he'd ever realized. He wasn't going to make a jerk of himself—for nothing—or was it nothing? His whole future was at stake.

"Rick, wait a second!" a voice called from behind him. He turned around to watch Joany drift up the stairs toward him. "I bought something for you," she said, indicating a package she held under her arm, strapped to her books. "But you can't peek until class."

Rick was too astonished to speak.

"Where's mine?" B.R. acted hurt.

"Sorry, B.R., but his isn't a free-for-nothing gift. Rick earned his."

"I did?"

"Sure. I think you're very noble for taking a class in home economics. Most guys think they're too good for it, or that it's something that only females would be interested in. We girls think you're impressively open-minded."

"You do?"

"That's right. In fact, this present isn't only from me. Peggy, Mary and Tera chipped in, too. But I got to pick it out." She reached up and patted Rick's arm, causing his heart to accelerate. "We're really proud of you, Rick."

"Yeah," B.R. agreed. "That Rick is one liberated guy. No false pride or chauvinistic bones in his body! He's every inch equal opportunity."

Rick shot a warning glance.

"Well, I've got to see a teacher before first period." Joany turned toward the door, and Rick hastily opened it for her. "Now remember, don't peek until class," she reminded him as she waved goodbye.

Rick watched her disappear among the mass of bodies that formed the two rivers flowing up and down the hall. He switched his books in his hands once more and started after the trail of her embracing perfume.

"Hey, where are you going?" B.R. asked. "If you want to withdraw from home ec, you have to go to the administration office. The other way!"

"I'm not going to drop out anymore," Rick replied. "Every inch of me is equal opportunity now. See ya."

B.R. chuckled and headed the opposite direction to his own first-period class. "Women," he muttered. "What they can do to a guy!"

"All right, class," Mrs. Bristol began. "As I promised, Mondays have become our quiz day. I've prepared a short test over our equipment and how it's used. There will be a few questions on nutrition, and on page two I expect everyone to write a one-paragraph explanation of how one would concoct a nice, stiff mixture of meringue. Are there any questions?" Her narrow, black eyes scanned the room. Bullets searching for target.

Uneasily Rick raised his hand.

"Yes, Mr. Masterson, what is it?"

"Are we allowed to use our recipe books to double-check the ingredients of the meringue?"

A light wave of giggles washed over the room.

"No, Mr. Masterson. If I allowed everyone to use their cook books, it would be a joke, not a test." She cleared her throat, putting a stop to any remaining laughter. "Most of you should complete the quiz before the class has ended. If so, you may sit at the tables in the back and talk quietly. Now, may I have a volunteer to pass out the tests?"

Rick's arm shot up. He thought he saw Mrs. Bristol roll her eyes, but he wasn't sure. She probably classed his constant willingness to help in the same category as Wolf's, who'd been trying to worm his way into her favor in the hopes of never having to work in class. Wolf figured you can't flunk someone you like. Thus his main goal for the semester was to get Mrs. Bristol to like him.

"Mr. Masterson, what a pleasant surprise," Mrs. Bristol said. "Here they are."

Shaking off what he detected as a note of sarcasm, Rick walked to her desk and picked up the neat stack of papers. He couldn't let little things, such as a teacher's questionable affection for him, deter his quest for a good grade. He smiled at her in his most charming way, still optomistic that she might someday change her opinion of him.

One corner of her mouth quivered slightly, as if a nerve had suffered a brief spasm. Not exactly the endearing benevolence he'd been hoping for.

"Make sure everyone has both pages," she said.

"Yes, ma'am."

Rick hurried to his seat as soon as the last page was handed out. Even though Mrs. Bristol had said most of the students would be able to finish the test before the period ended, he was worried about time. Her words "most of" really translated into, "All of you except the two stubble-faced creatures in the front row."

Surprisingly, the first half of the quiz went very rapidly. Many of the questions were about nutrition; the main food groups and vitamins that are needed to sustain a healthy body. The material had been taken from their class textbook, *Food and You*, which Rick had fervently studied over the weekend before he'd decided to drop the course.

The second half was more difficult. It had been worked up from class lectures and centered around the different appliances that covered the countertops. And then, as promised, came the essay question on the making of meringue.

Six egg whites. Rick would never forget that part as long as he lived. But he couldn't recall, without some trace of doubt, how much sugar was needed.

## The New Man

And that white stuff? Crème de Menthe... cream soda... Artificial cream? Johnson and Johnson bath powder?

No. That's only what it looked like. Tartar something...

Rick's forehead began to break into pinhead-size drops of sweat. His hands felt as though he'd washed them in clam dip. He took a dishcloth from the nearest countertop drawer and mopped his brow.

"I trust you're going to take that home and wash it before you use it again," Mrs. Bristol, who'd been pacing the floor on the alert for cheating, said from behind him.

He jumped, his hand jerking a pencil line across his test page. "Yes, ma'am. I'll be sure and do that," he said.

Several heads, including Joany's, looked up at him. Wiping his palms on the frilly-looking hand cloth, he hastily stuffed it inside his notebook.

Finally Rick had what he thought might be an accurate list of ingredients and the proper coinciding directions to make a "stiff" batch of meringue. Now he needed a month's rest. A medal. Several days of fishing.

Instead he took the package Joany had given him and walked to the back of the room. He noticed that half of the class was still at their desks, their heads bent over the test. It was a pleasant feeling realizing that he'd rated average at completing his test. The way he'd been feeling about himself and the chances he'd have of winning the Young Miss Homemaker Scholarship, he needed all the encouragement he could get.

"How did you do?" Joany whispered, waving for him to come and sit down beside her.

"Fine," he whispered back. "Was that white stuff called cream mint, or cream of tartar?"

"Cream of tartar."

"Oh, good, I got it right."

Suddenly, to Rick's ultimate pleasure and surprise, Joany's soft lips were on his cheek. He was enchanted by the gesture. It sent his pulse racing. His mind whirling. He felt like dropping to his knee and begging for her hand in marriage. They could be wed at lunchtime. Before his physics class.

Who needed a medal, a month's rest or a three-day fishing trip when you could have a honeymoon? With Joany?

She pulled away, and his mind began to function again. If he so much as moved one inch closer to her, Mrs. Bristol would be after him.

"I think you're so intellectual, Rick," she said. "I really do."

"Thank you, Joany." Did she realize he wanted to swoop her onto a spirited white horse and carry her across campus into the sunset? Could she see his heart swell with hope or his eyes shine with affection?

"Why don't you open your present?"

"Okay. Sure."

She scooted her chair closer, causing his pulse to plummet into the thousands again. "I really hope you like it."

"If you picked it out, I'm sure I will."

He glanced into her eyes as he tore the tape off the package. She reassured him with her straight mint smile. Everything was fine.

The paper opened up into a patch of blue. It was material, a sheer, frilly kind of cloth. It could only be a handkerchief. But what a strange-looking handkerchief! Was it perhaps a scarf? He pulled the entire piece of material into view.

It was an apron. It had ruffled shoulders and a big bow, and lettering over the pockets that read, Domestic Engineer.

"Do you like it?" Joany asked.

Rick couldn't answer.

"We noticed that you didn't have one last Friday. I picked a blue one because I thought it would look good with your hair color. Come on, tell me what you think. Are you surprised?"

"Mmm."

"Well try it on. We want to see what it looks like." She glanced around at several of her friends who'd scooted their chairs in to join the conversation. They giggled. All eyes were on Rick.

He sucked in a breath. Lifting one of the frilly arm loops open, he started to stick his large hand through.

At the very last second, as though he were an amateur sky diver trying to figure out how to escape his first soaring jump earthward, Rick hesitated. He surveyed the pretty, waiting faces around him.

If only he knew how to dematerialize. Deport himself to a hole somewhere. The last thing in the world he wanted to do was disappoint Joany. Yet he couldn't do it. He wound the fluff of cloth into a haphazard bundle and tossed it onto the table.

Joany's expression was a mixture of hurt and confusion. In that split second Rick realized that he had never seen Joany upset before. She'd always acted happy and so considerate of the people around her.

"What's the matter?" she demanded. "We all have one. Mrs. Bristol suggested them to protect our clothes from stains."

"Yes, I know, but you guys are supposed to wear them. I mean, they were made for you."

"Oh, really."

Rick never knew such a nice girl could look so mean. He couldn't remember her ever being so threatening in elementary school or junior high.

"What I mean to say is that an apron belongs on a girl."

"And boys are too good for them?"

"I didn't say that."

"But that's what you meant, wasn't it?"

"No. Aprons are nice. There's nothing wrong with them."

"As long as they hang on the right sex!" Her brown eyes turned black.

"Did I hear my favorite subject?" Wolf interrupted, lifting himself to plop on the table in front of them. He grinned at Joany. "How'd you do on the test, Joany-Oany?"

"Fine, Wolf."

"Then why the frown?"

## The New Man

"It's Rick. We bought him an apron, and he doesn't want to wear it."

Wolf's eyes gleamed as he studied the circle of people around him. He zeroed in on Joany with her frustrated, pouty expression, and Rick with his desperate one.

"Why won't you wear the apron, Rick?" he asked.

"Because it's not for me," Rick answered shortly.

"He thinks he's too good for it." Joany shook her head in disgust. "He's a chauvinist. I'll bet his mother has to wait on him hand and foot."

"Give him a break, Joany," another girl cut in. "Probably he's embarrassed because it's so frilly."

"Yeah," another friend agreed. "Perhaps Rick would feel better if we exchanged it for a plain, white one. You know, the sort the chefs always wear."

"That's the kind I would've bought. Not such a dainty one."

"Me, too. Did you really check around, Joany?"

She turned to glare at them. "Of course, I didn't. If this apron is good enough for any of us, then it should be fine for him, too."

"I think you're making it into too big of an issue. Rick's not a chauvinist. He just doesn't want to wear girls' stuff." The girls looked at each other and nodded in agreement.

Wolf scanned the eyes of the girls. They were intent, waiting. Clearly needing a hero to step in. "No big deal," he mumbled to himself. He situated the fabric over his chest and asked Joany to tie it for him. "There. You see, Rick? It's only an apron. Nothing to get bent out of shape about." He turned to Joany. "And it's such a nice color, too. The style would've looked great on ya, Rick. Did you pick it out, Joany?"

"Yes."

"Well, I think you have good taste. And it was very thoughtful of you, too."

"The other girls chipped in with me," Joany admitted. Her eyes narrowed. "I propose we give the apron to Wolf since Rick doesn't like it."

The others exchanged unsure expressions. "I don't know, Joany," someone objected. "That's not what we originally agreed to do. We chipped in to buy an apron for Rick, not Wolf."

"Yes, but Rick won't wear it, so what does it matter? Wolf deserves it more."

Wolf bowed his head in pretend humbleness.

"Well, it would be a shame to have it sit around unused," one girl finally relented.

"If Wolf will really use it, why not?" another agreed.

Shortly after, to Rick's extreme relief, the bell rang, and everyone had to rush off to the third-period class.

Wolf walked with him from the room, pausing before they reached the door. He hurriedly stuffed the apron out of sight, beneath his shirt. "Tough break, eh, Rick?" he said, patting at the bulk of material so that it would look like a normal part of his body.

"What are you doing that for?"

"You don't expect me to let anyone see this dumb-looking thing do you?"

"But you acted as though you didn't mind wearing it in front of the girls."

"Of course. Do you think I'm crazy? You saw them. They were ready to lynch you. Besides, babe-of-my-heart Joany-Oany was impressed by my sophisticated attitude." He pretended to straighten an invisible tie. "She likes a man with an open mind."

"Yours is open all right," Rick growled. "There's air from ear to ear."

"You're just jealous. Everyone knows you've always liked Joany." He moved his head back and forth, trying to locate her among the bodies ahead of them.

Rick felt the back of his neck prick hotly as Wolf socked him in the shoulder.

"Don't be sore, but like I said, Joany won't be able to think about anyone else but yours truly by the end of the semester. Women are like putty when it comes to the Wolf."

"Aren't you late for an appointment somewhere? Maybe a window that needs breaking or tires to flatten?"

"No need for hostility. I'm on my way." He whistled at a passing girl before he jogged ahead, zigzagging through the crowd. "Later, partner," he yelled over his shoulder.

Rick continued to float along with the stream of bodies, his mind wandering back to the horrible scene he'd just suffered through.

Mostly, he was confused. Joany had kissed him today, the first time since they'd been children in the third grade when he had given her all his solid-colored marbles because she'd said they were pretty. Less than fifteen minutes ago, he'd felt like the man who'd finally found the end of the rainbow, the most fortunate guy in the universe.

Then the crash. He could kick himself for having acted so stupid! If only he didn't have such a complex about trying to win a girl's scholarship! If the Young Miss Homemaker title had only been formed to sound less feminine. Something like the Young Mr. Male or Miss Female Person's Homemaker Scholarship or Money Fund for the Desperate and Needy; the Scholarship for Both Sexes! He wouldn't have been nearly as self-conscious about putting on the apron. He could've handled his predicament in a more mature way.

He didn't really feel that he was too good to wear an apron or that cooking was only for girls. He had the highest respect for women and had never underestimated their capabilities or intelligence.

But now Joany thought that he was a narrow-minded chauvinist who judged women to be second-class citizens. How far from the truth! Take her for example. Rick considered Joany first-rate, more noble and bright and honest than any of his friends.

Aprons! He wanted to stuff them all down Wolf's throat. That king of sleaze was the real chauvinist! He thought of women as simple, frail victims that could be maneuvered, tricked and manipulated into doing his will.

To even think that someone like Joany could ever fall for a guy like him! How preposterous! There was a better possibility of a butterfly falling in love with a frog!

Tomorrow he would pull Joany to the side and explain to her why he was taking home economics and the reasons for his stubborn oversensitivity about wearing aprons. It would take a lot of courage on his part. But he decided it would be worth any momentary discomfort. He had confidence that a girl like Joany would understand his situation. She would probably be able to help him in his attitude, too, and maybe even give him advice.

"Hey, partner!" Rick heard a familiar voice above the locker-slamming clatter of the hall. He spotted Wolf leaning against the wall. His heart dropped like a barrel of cement when he noticed who was standing beside him. Unlikely as it seemed, the frog was now within inches of the butterfly.

Wolf read Rick's expression and grinned. He had his arms outstretched, and Joany was pulling books from her locker, piling them on him.

Rick looked quickly away and hastened his walk, pretending to be in a sudden hurry to get somewhere else.

Some things were just too difficult to face.

## Chapter Four

"Don't worry about the dishes, Mom, we'll get them." Rick hopped up from the table and busied himself collecting soiled plates and glasses.

B.R. stared at him, as much in shock as Rick's parents. He'd been coming to the Mastersons' home for supper ever since he could remember, and never, not even in jest, had Rick ever volunteered to do the dishes. "I thought guests were supposed to relax after their meal and throw gracious compliments to the hostess."

"You're not a guest. You're a bean pole, deeply in debt to this lady for filling your belly with a great supper."

"Rick!" his mother said. "Don't be rude to B.R. He doesn't owe us a thing for his meal."

"No, Mrs. Masterson, Rick's got a point, tactless as he may be. I do appreciate your cooking, and I should show my gratitude by helping with this after-dinner catastrophe."

"That's right, Mom." Rick slid his father's plate off of the table. "There's no rule that says we can't help you with the kitchen work."

"I know, Ricky, but you do so much for me already. You keep the yard looking so neat and the cars running, and you take out the gar—"

"All things that are considered men's work. I want to broaden my horizons. I don't want anyone to accuse me of letting you wait on me hand and foot."

"But they already have," B.R. pointed out.

Rick jabbed his elbow into B.R.'s stomach, causing him to wheeze out air. "Well, then, I don't want the rumor to spread any further."

"I think there's more to this than meets the eye," Mr. Masterson observed, studying the two boys skeptically.

"Well, I'm not looking a gift horse in the mouth. In fact, I kind of like the idea of men doing the dishes. Or at least helping we women with them if they haven't got anything more important to do." Mrs. Masterson gave her husband a long obvious stare.

"Thanks, Rick," he said dryly. "I just love it when you bring your theories into our once-happy home."

"Really, Herbert, is there anything wrong with helping your wife with such a simple chore?" Mrs. Masterson asked.

"No, honey. I like doing things that make you happy," Mr. Masterson said, collecting the remaining silverware. "Perhaps I should consider editing the dinner conversations in future. Rick can tell me what he plans to say during the meal, and then I could tie a scarf around his mouth and feed him intravenously."

"Don't pay any attention to your father," Mrs. Masterson said. "He's just envious because you had the idea of helping me first."

"That's right, Rick. All these years I've been secretly yearning for dishpan hands, but I didn't know how I could break out of my tedious rut of relaxing in my easy chair to read the evening paper every night. Now I have you to thank for setting me free." He paused. "Thanks again, Rick."

"No problem, Pop." Rick grinned at him. "Someday I'm really going to shake up the house. I'm going to make dessert!"

"How nice!" Mrs. Masterson clasped her hands together. "What will it be?"

"Lemon meringue pie."

"Tell me, son, why all the adventure?" Mr. Masterson added two gummy forks to his collection of tableware.

"If I explained, Dad, it would only increase your blood pressure."

"Would it help me to cope with these little surprises?"

"It might aid you in understanding them."

"Then I think it's worth the risk of a heart attack. Go ahead and tell me."

"I gotta run." B.R. unloaded his pile of napkins and bread crusts in the garbage and waved a hasty goodbye.

"Hold up, Bones. This whole thing was your idea."

"No it wasn't. *It was your idea.*"

"Yeah, like elephants chirp."

"Blaming your problems on other people is a coward's way out."

"Is that why you're headed for the door?"

Mr. Masterson pounded the table with his fist full of tableware. "Okay, boys. I'm not getting one thing from this conversation. You're going to have to clue me in on what 'idea' you're talking about. Rick, since you're the person who's been living in my house longer, why don't you do the talking?"

"Yes, Dad." He grabbed one of B.R.'s belt loops and yanked him to the table into his seat. "It's all got to do with education." He lifted his chin. "You know how I would like to get a job working with computers?"

Mr. Masterson nodded.

"Well, you need to obtain a college degree to do that."

Mr. Masterson nodded again.

"And you need to obtain money to obtain a college degree."

"Yes, son."

"Lots of money."

Mr. Masterson smacked his forehead in pretend amazement. "You're a walking encyclopedia, Rick."

"It takes more money than I've been able to save up."

"And how much have you been able to save up?"

"One hundred thirty seven dollars."

"But what about all your jobs? You've been working on a college fund since you were in sixth grade. You could've been independently wealthy by now!"

"It went into the truck, Dad, which, by the way, should be running nicely for another century or so."

Rick had toiled and saved until his account had reached a high of nearly seventeen hundred dollars. It hadn't been his fault that his truck had cost almost fifteen hundred dollars to buy, repair and keep in working order.

"But I don't want you to worry," he continued determinedly. "There's a scholarship that I might be qualified for. B.R. and I have looked it over extremely carefully, and we think I have a good chance of getting it."

"And what scholarship is this, son?" his mom asked.

B.R. covered his eyes.

Rick swallowed.

"The Young Miss Homemaker Scholarship."

His mother dropped back onto her chair. She and his dad exchanged this deep, are-you-thinking-what-I'm-thinking look that longtime mates do instead of talking. Rick had always thought his parents were superb at this peculiar exhibition of mind sharing. Their

## The New Man

stares could run into a full minute, and then, at the end of it all, they'd both turn to Rick, and one would speak, the other in perfect agreement with whatever was said.

Like now. Their eye contact broken, they were now both studying him. It appeared that it was his father who was going to do the talking.

"Forgive me if I seem presumptuous, but doesn't the word 'Miss' indicate someone of the female sex?" he asked quietly.

"Yes, but that's not what the rules say. They're stated so that the sex of their homemakers doesn't matter."

"That's right," B.R. cut in. "And Rick is just as much female as anyone else, anyway."

"Thanks, Buddy." Rick rolled his eyes. "What B.R. is so crudely trying to say is that we think I'm capable of learning all the requirements needed to win the scholarship. And since they say boys can be qualified for it the same as girls, there's no reason why I shouldn't at least try." He paused a moment. "It's for two thousand dollars."

At least he'd said it. Now he would have to follow through with it. There could be no more indecisiveness or spontaneous attempts to withdraw from his homemaking courses. He was chained to his goal. The only path before him now led to blenders, stoves, ovens and aprons. His parents would have to accept his decision for better or for worse....

By the end of the evening he had convinced them.

"Attention class," Mrs. Bristol began. "I have several announcements I would like to make. First of all, I'll be turning last Monday's test papers back to you. I'll need a volunteer, please."

Rick didn't get his hand up fast enough. He heard Mrs. Bristol call on Wolf. "All right, Mr. D'Antonio. Please step to the desk."

Rick slumped in his chair, a beaten man. Passing out papers had been his last hope of conveying his message to Joany. She wouldn't have been able to avoid him then. He could've mouthed the words "I'm sorry" to her as she reached for her test.

"Here, partner." Wolf interrupted his thoughts, and pressed a sheet of paper in his hand. "Next time we ought to confer a little during the quiz. I barely pulled a *D*."

When Rick looked at the top of the page and saw the circled *A* with the words "one hundred percent" marked beside it, he almost let out a war whoop. He wanted to leap for joy and hop around the room like a mad kangaroo. All thoughts of Joany were momentarily pushed aside as he reveled in his unexpected success. This was the first concrete sign that all his hard work and sacrifice was actually doing some good. It was the first valid indication that he might really be able to pull off the impossible and win the scholarship.

He couldn't wait to show his parents, and B.R., and maybe even Joany? He glanced at her, and his heart drummed with a surge of hope. He'd caught her watching him. She looked away immediately, pretending that she'd only been brushing something from her shoulder. It wasn't exactly the most encouraging signal of love, but at least she still realized he was alive.

"Secondly, I'd like to report that we have a dish towel missing. I've worked very hard to get the funding for the equipment and supplies for this course. I'm leaving it up to your personal honor to return the property that has mysteriously disappeared from this classroom. No charges will be raised against the thief."

"Who is she kidding?" Wolf hid his snickering behind the palm of his hand. "Someone took a dumb towel, and she's acting like the Mafia stole a car. Grand-larceny charges for missing terry cloth. What a riot!"

Rick was already in a great mood because of his test grade, not to mention the wonderful fact that he'd caught Joany looking at him. So when Mrs. Bristol gave her speech about the towel, there was nothing he could do but laugh. Who would ever take a dumb dishcloth? Who would even want it? She was acting so serious about something so trivial, it had to be funny.

He reached beneath his desk to fish his home-ec notebook from his other things. Mrs. Bristol had abandoned her topic of criminal injustice and was moving into a brief lecture on the "merits of Mr. Potato." If he expected to continue his good grade average, he would need to keep taking complete notes.

He opened the hard-surfaced cover, glanced inside, then slammed it shut again. He made such an abrupt noise, three people turned to look at him. Mrs. Bristol paused for several oxygen-stopping seconds. She waited until she was sure the commotion was incidental, and not intentional, and then continued.

Slowly, with as little movement as he could manage, Rick cracked his notebook enough to peek inside again.

It wasn't his imagination after all. There was a real live dish towel stuffed in his big-ringed notebook. Mrs. Bristol's missing equipment. He suddenly remembered that she'd told him to take it home and wash it when she'd seen him wipe the perspiration from his face during the test. But, after the ordeal with the apron, and because he'd never gotten into his home-ec notebook since Monday, he'd forgotten all about it.

It wasn't simply a sweaty dishcloth anymore. It was evidence, and he was a criminal.

"Mr. Potato is a misunderstood little fellow. People think he's high in calories, but considering his protein content, he's really quite efficient. It's not the little fellow himself who's fattening but the things people stuff him with. Actually he's economical and rich in vitamins and minerals."

Rick inspected her face, a lightly rouged mask, trying to figure out her motive for announcing the stolen dishcloth. Why was it such a big deal to her? Surely the cost of one dish towel wouldn't strain the budget that much.

By the time the bell rang he was pretty sure that she'd honestly forgotten her previous instructions to him, which meant he should make a clean breast of things and remind her of who had her towel. He was

**Enjoy reading about yourself and your friends in First Love from Silhouette**

# Every one a good story... Get 4 FREE novels and

**get more great First Love from Silhouette® novels
—for a 15-day FREE examination—
delivered to your door every month!**

First Love from Silhouette novels are about girls...and guys...you know or would like to meet. They're about things that matter to you, they capture your thoughts and your feelings.

As a member of the First Love from Silhouette home subscription service, you can get these exciting books delivered right to your door. You'll always be among the first to get them, and you'll never miss a single title!

## FREE BOOKS

Start today by taking advantage of this special offer—4 new First Love from Silhouette novels (a $7.80 Value) *absolutely FREE,* along with a free Mystery Gift. Just fill out and mail the attached order card.

## AT-HOME PREVIEWS, FREE DELIVERY

Once you receive your 4 free books, you'll have the chance to preview 4 more First Love from Silhouette novels every month —*as soon as they are published!* When you decide to keep them, you'll pay just $7.80, *with no additional charges of any kind and at no risk!*

Cancel your subscription at any time simply by dropping us a note. In any case, the first 4 books and Mystery Gift are yours to keep.

## EXTRA BONUS

When you take advantage of this special offer, we'll also send you the First Love from Silhouette Newsletter FREE with each shipment. Each issue features news on future titles and interviews with your favorite authors.

# Get a FREE Mystery Gift, too!

**EVERY BOOK YOU RECEIVE WILL BE A BRAND-NEW FULL-LENGTH NOVEL!**

**CLIP AND MAIL THIS POSTPAID CARD TODAY!**

NO POSTAGE NECESSARY IF MAILED IN THE UNITED STATES

## BUSINESS REPLY CARD
FIRST CLASS  PERMIT NO. 194  CLIFTON, N.J.

*Postage will be paid by addressee*

**Silhouette Books
120 Brighton Road
P.O. Box 5084
Clifton, NJ 07015-9956**

# Enjoy 4 First Love from Silhouette novels (a $7.80 Value) FREE and get a Mystery Gift, too!

## First Love from Silhouette®

**Silhouette Books, 120 Brighton Rd., P.O. Box 5084, Clifton, NJ 07015-9956**

Yes, please send me FREE and without obligation, the 4 newest First Love from Silhouette novels along with my Mystery Gift. Unless you hear from me after I receive my 4 FREE books, please send me 4 more First Love from Silhouette novels for a free 15-day examination each month as soon as they are published.

I understand that you will bill me a total of just $7.80, with no additional charges of any kind. There is no minimum number of books that I must buy, and I can cancel at any time. The first 4 books and Mystery Gift are mine to keep, even if I never take a single additional book.

NAME _____
(please print)

ADDRESS _____

CITY _____ STATE ____ ZIP ____

Terms and prices subject to change. Your enrollment is subject to acceptance by Silhouette Books.
FIRST LOVE FROM SILHOUETTE is a registered trademark.

CTF855

hoping any anger she might feel would be replaced with relief of locating her property.

He waited until everyone—including Joany—had left, and Mrs. Bristol was back at her desk. He collected his belongings and walked toward her.

"Mrs. Bristol?"

"Yes, Mr. Masterson?"

"Um, you know about the towel thing."

"Yes, Mr. Masterson."

"I happen to know where it is."

"Good, Mr. Masterson. Where?"

He opened his home-ec notebook. "It's not what you think, though. I can explain what happened."

Her eyes became smaller. Closer. She was the only human being he'd ever known who could do such extraordinary things with their permanent bone structure. "I'm listening, Mr. Masterson."

"Do you remember last Monday when you told me to take the towel home and wash it after I wiped my sweat on it?"

"Mmm. Vaguely, Mr. Masterson."

"Well, I put it in my notebook to take it with me, and I forgot about it."

"I see, Mr. Masterson."

"Yes, ma'am." He reached the wadded-up towel across the desk. "I'd like to return it to you now."

"Ugh. Please follow my original instructions first, Mr. Masterson."

"Oh, right. And I'll use bleach and hot water. I realize you need them for bright colors."

She frowned. "Don't you watch commercials, Mr. Masterson? Bleach and hot water should be used with white materials and fabrics that won't run."

"Run?" He stuffed the towel back into his notebook. "Where?"

"Good day, Mr. Masterson."

"Goodbye, Mrs. Bristol."

## Chapter Five

Rick met Clara, the other worker at Humpty Dump-All Nursery School. Though she was firmer than a police squad with the kids, she was extremely friendly and helpful to Rick.

She instructed him on how to gain control over children without throwing little red fire engines against the wall to get their attention. She explained how he could tell if a child needed a bathroom break before it was too late and what to do should he need to dislodge a foreign object from one of the toilet bowls.

Heidi said she was surprised to see him again.

"No offense, Rick," she'd admitted after blowing wisps of hair from her face. "But I didn't think you would show. I figured you would see what it was like in a zoo of thumb suckers, and make like vapor. I mean, I expect raises every now and then to give me the inspiration to show up in the mornings. And you're doing it free."

Rick enjoyed the way Clara and Heidi were looking at him, and he didn't want to ruin their impressions with a lot of confusing facts. They saw him as a self-sacrificing hero who put the needs of others before his own interests. They continued on about how grateful they were that he had come again and said how hard it was to find a responsible volunteer like him. He basked in their praise.

And then there were the kids themselves. He was amazed that so many of them had remembered him from the week before. Little red-haired Sarah walked right up and said, "Hewo, Mistur Wick. I wuv you way up to da sky. Wanna play wiff me?" And Stevie, the stuttering blond boy, insisted on calling him mommy. Heidi was finally able to convince him to use another title, Captain Rick, which most of the other kids quickly adopted, too.

Rick felt pretty good about his job, and when five o'clock came, a part of him actually wanted to stay. It was a great feeling to be needed. Before he walked to the closet to get his shoes that he'd taken off for another hyped-up game of ring-around-the-rosy, he paused to gaze over the sun-filled room. Humming to himself, he slipped his foot into a shoe.

Something most unnatural was in the bottom of his sneaker. It squished when he applied pressure. He took it off and peered inside. Someone had added two tablespoons of peanut butter to his shoe. His ears reddened with anger. Slipping off his sock, he scanned the room. He zeroed in on a large-size boy who was banging a doll against the wall.

*Beany D'Antonio.*

"Don't try nuthin' with me crumb head," the scowling boy was yelling to the doll. "Next time I'll zap you with my laser and throw you to my giant frog. Understand you stupid girl?"

Clara clucked disapprovingly as she surveyed the mushy sock. "Remember, Rick, no spanking. It's not allowed," she reminded him.

"Friendly firmness and isolation," Heidi added, coming to join them.

"I'm going to roll him up in a little 'Beany ball' and bounce him off the wall."

"Uh-uh, Rick. That's not allowed, either."

"I'm going to hang him by his toes and twist him around until he looks like a screw."

"You shouldn't threaten."

"A pogo-stick coil."

"You're not listening."

He turned to the women and asked, "Do either of you have a hairbrush?"

They exchanged glances. "It's been a long day, Rick," Clara said tentatively. "Why don't you go ahead and go home. Heidi and I will take care of things here. We can handle Beany for you."

"Only if you promise to make him suffer. Otherwise I'm staying."

"Now, Rick, we know you don't mean that."

"You're right. I don't mean that. Beany is only a little kid. He doesn't really know what he's doing."

"I warned you stupid underwear face. You're through now!"

Abruptly Beany swung the doll like a baseball bat against the hard block wall. It's plastic, blond head went spiraling across the floor.

Sarah recognized it as it rolled past her, and her round green eyes swelled with tears. "Baby Betsy!" she cried out. "Who hewt my Baby Betsy?" She abandoned her pile of building blocks to run after the rolling head. Several more girls, who were also part-time mothers to Baby Betsy, chased after her screaming and shouting.

Instantly the room was in chaos.

"Beany, come here!" Clara commanded, starting toward Beany.

Heidi grabbed hold of two boys as they headed over to join the mob. "Go on home, Rick. We'll take care of things. If you get involved now, you'll end up staying another hour."

"But I can't abandon ship like this."

"Sure you can. Clara and I have riot control down to a fine art."

Rick glanced at little Sarah who was cradling Baby Betsy. "Maybe I could help calm Sarah down. Take her outside or something."

"That would be okay, except her aunt should be picking her up any minute." She waved Rick away. "Just go on home and don't worry. Most of the parents will be here within the next half hour."

Rick finally gave in, shrugging. "Okay. See you next Friday."

"Right. And don't forget your sock."

"Right." Gingerly he picked up the gooey remains of his footwear and headed out the door.

When Rick walked into Mr. Ryan's insurance office, he saw Joany sitting on one of the black couches in the paneled lobby. Their looks connected for a split second, then jerked away like fingers that had touched fire.

His heart thudded wildly in his chest. His mind whirled with all the possible reasons of why she was there, hoping desperately that what he finally concluded would be wrong.

Rick knew it wasn't, though. At the beginning of the class that day, Mrs. Bristol had announced that those interested in applying for the Young Miss Homemaker award could pick up their applications at Mr. Ryan's insurance office.

It had never occurred to Rick that Joany might run for the Young Miss Homemaker Scholarship, too. He cringed at what her reaction would be when she found out that they were both running for the same award. There was little doubt her feelings for him would change from indifference to dislike. She'd consider him a hypocrite; the king of deception... the master of bad surprises.

A real crumb.

He couldn't blame her, either. She was going to find out about everything in the worst way possible. The news would hit her like a bombshell, and he'd have no time to soften the shock of it. She'd never know why he was doing something so crazy, and she would be hurt that he'd never trusted her enough to explain it. He simply couldn't let her find out about it! Not like this.

He walked up to Mr. Ryan's secretary with a pleasant smile.

"I'm here to see Mr. Ryan, ma'am."

"So is the young lady on the couch, and Mr. Ryan is with someone at the moment. Could I help you with something?"

"No, ma'am."

"Is this concerning auto, life or fire insurance?"

"I'm not sure yet."

"I see. When do you think you'll know?"

"Later. Perhaps when it's my turn to see Mr. Ryan." He purposefully kept his voice low.

"All right. We'll just wait. May I have your name?"

"Rick Masterson."

"Middle initial?"

"It doesn't matter."

She nodded. "Okay, Rick. Please take a seat. Mr. Ryan will be out in about fifteen minutes, which should give you plenty of time to remember why you're here."

"Thank you."

He took the seat farthest from Joany, knowing without looking up that the secretary was still watching him with curiosity.

"Hi, Rick," Joany said.

## The New Man

"Hi, Joany. I'm here on personal business with Mr. Ryan," he quickly said.

Joany looked at him curiously. "I'm here to get an application for the Young Miss Homemaker Scholarship. I suppose you consider it a silly award." She looked at him defiantly.

"Two thousand bucks? Are you kidding?" he exclaimed without thinking.

"You know how much it's for?"

"Sure." He straightened his collar and pressed at his buttons nervously. "I don't think it's a silly award, either. I'll bet whoever gets it will have earned it with a lot of hard work and dedication."

Joany's brown eyes shone with surprise. "Do you really mean that?"

"Sure. I have a mother. I can see how hard it is to do all that stuff."

Joany continued to regard him thoughtfully. "But, of course, you'd never consider involving yourself in 'all that stuff' seeing as how you're a *man*."

"Sure I would. If no one did that work, we'd all live in dumps, eat potato chips for dinner every night and have maladjusted children. Personally, I really hope to have a big part in helping my wife when I get married."

Had he gone too far?

Joany's expression softened. "I think that's a wonderful way to look at life, Rick. Very mature and thoughtful. So why didn't you put on my apron?"

"I thought I would look like a sissy," he confessed.

"But that's silly!"

"I know that now."

"Do you think about marriage very often, Rick? I mean, like what you want it to be like?"

"Sometimes. I think a person should plan for it and inform himself on how to help the marriage commitment last and what makes certain relationships more successful than others. I think it's only sensible for a young person to educate himself about something so important as his future."

Both the secretary and Joany were staring at him openmouthed. Although he'd gotten what he'd just said from the front of a marriage book in the dean's office, he believed every word of it.

But judging from their dumbfounded expression, he'd carried his sales pitch a bit too far. He'd only meant to prove to Joany that he wasn't a thickheaded chauvinist.

"Young man," the well-groomed secretary interrupted. "That's a very astute and well-developed observation. I couldn't help overhearing, and I must say, I'm in full agreement with you."

"Me, too." Joany's cheeks turned a darker color.

"You know, if more men had your outlook on life, there wouldn't be nearly as many divorces and separations," the secretary began, but was interrupted by her phone ringing. She pushed a few buttons on the phone panel, then buzzed Mr. Ryan on the intercom. Placing the receiver back, she explained to Joany.

"I'm sorry, dear, but a small emergency has come up. Is there anything I can help you with?"

## The New Man

"Our teacher at school said we could pick up applications for the young Miss Homemaker Scholarship here," Joany explained.

"Oh, good grief! You should've told me sooner!" She beamed. "I'll take care of you right away." She opened her desk drawer and pulled out several papers. "My name is Sally, and I'm the treasurer of the Redona Society of American Homemakers. It's nice to meet you, Joany. I'm pleased to have you as one of our candidates."

They shook hands.

The front door opened, and several more girls from school walked in. They all greeted Joany and then said hi to Rick when they noticed he was in the lobby, too. He nodded back at them, trying not to look guilty. Three more Young Miss Homemaker candidates joined the others, adding to the confusion.

Rick felt a tugging at his heart as he noticed how Joany was becoming so wrapped up in talking to her friends about the scholarship. It sounded as though she was as hopeful about winning as he was.

Worse yet, she seemed to have completely forgotten that he was there. She placed her hand on the door, but at the last second she turned to him and said, "It was wonderful talking with you, Rick."

Her friends giggled. His ears felt hot.

"It was nice talking to you, too, Joany."

"If you ever need any help with your home-ec homework, just let me know."

Rick was acutely conscious of the other girls' grins. He felt a ripple of yellow cowardice creep up his spine.

With as much poise as he could muster, he said, "Okay, sounds good." He breathed a sigh of relief when they followed Joany out the door. Glancing around the room, he made doubly sure everyone had left before he approached Sally's desk. "Ma'am," he said, "can you please help me?"

"I'd be glad to," she said pleasantly. "What can I do?"

Rick felt his words catch in his throat. "May I... may I have an application for the Young Miss Homemaker Scholarship, please?"

"For your sister?"

"No, ma'am. For me."

"Are you serious?"

"Yes, ma'am. The rules state that boys are qualified to run, also."

"Well, you're correct there. In fact it was my idea to extend the rules to include males. I did it to be fair, although I really didn't think anyone would actually be interested." She reached her hand out, and Rick shook it. "You're quite a young man, Mr. Masterson."

"Not really, ma'am."

"But I do wish you had spoken up. I've handed all the applications out. I wasn't expecting such a large group all at once. I have an idea, though." She quickly found her pad and pen and began scribbling on it. "Isabel," she explained glancing up at him, "our president, has some copies. I'm sure she wouldn't mind if you stopped by her house and picked one up. I've written her address down on this slip of paper."

## The New Man

She handed it toward him. "I'll go ahead and call her and let her know you're on your way."

He smiled as he took the slip of paper. "Thank you, ma'am."

"You're welcome." Beaming, she shook his hand again. "I wish you the best, Rick. It's a pleasure to meet you. I wish there were more young men around today with your open-minded attitude."

Rick drove slowly down the street of well kept homes, trying to decode the faded numbers on the dusty curbs for Isabel's address. He was thinking about what Sally had said to him and wondering if he really had a chance of winning the award. For sure he would have to have a better grasp of cooking. He was still having difficulties in getting everything to turn out the way it was supposed to.

Part of the reason was that he had Wolf as his cooking partner. Take the time it had been "The Week of Mr. Potato." That Friday, when the class was commissioned to demonstrate the many uses of that "outstanding little vegetable," Wolf had volunteered himself and Rick for the category of mashed potatoes. Rick had planned on doing the category of baked potatoes instead, as they were much simpler: wash, prick, foil wrap and plop in the oven, but Wolf had stuck his big-knuckled hand into the air before Rick had the chance to stop him. He'd convinced Rick that he'd made mashed potatoes many times before, so when it came time to peel them, Rick believed Wolf's instructions that you should leave them in their jackets. They'd crushed the vegetables and then whipped them, fully dressed.

Tan slush with big brown lumps. It looked as though they'd scraped it off the front of a twelve-truck convoy. They couldn't even salvage a decent helping to show Mrs. Bristol. It seemed that each time he gained an inch with her, he'd slip back four feet more. He was positive that she neither liked nor trusted him. If she let personality differences affect his final grade in class, a sure factor in his qualifications for the Young Miss Homemaker Scholarship, he would be a goner. Any hope of winning the award would disintegrate like snow in an oven.

One thousand forty-four East Chestnut. The numbers were painted brightly on the mailbox. Vivid orange and yellow marigolds trailed both sides of the immaculate sidewalk that led to the porch. Healthy-looking asparagus ferns hung by macrames along the top eaves.

Rick rang the doorbell, whistling beneath his breath. There was a small cross-stitch sign hanging from below one of the larger macrames. It read, Good Cooks Are Like Artists. They Always Draw People.

An older man holding the evening newspaper in his hand opened the door. "What can I do for you son?" he asked, peaking over the top of his half-moon reading glasses.

"I'm here to see Isabel, sir."

"She's cooking my dinner right now. Can I help you with something?" he asked.

## The New Man

Rick shook his head. "I don't think so, sir. Sally from Mr. Ryan's insurance office told me that I need to pick something up from Isabel. It should only take a few seconds."

"All right, son. But Belle's makin' my favorite tonight." He rubbed his tight, round stomach. "Teriyaki Beef and Peppers. I've trusted students before and ended up with scrambled eggs and toast for supper. That would be a terrible letdown for a poor old fella expecting a savory Japanese cuisine." He winked. "But give me your word it'll be short, and I'll fetch her for you."

"You got it." Rick chuckled to himself as the older man disappeared. He began rocking on the balls of his feet, feeling exceedingly relieved that the officers of the Society of American Homemakers were so helpful and friendly.

A few seconds later the man's wife, Isabel, appeared.

Rick nearly tilted off balance, onto the lawn. He gathered the small amount of air remaining in his lungs and managed a weak-sounding greeting.

"Hello, Mrs. Bristol, President Isabel, ma'am."

"Good afternoon, Mr. Masterson," she replied. "Sally said you were coming. I must say, I'm amazed."

"Yes, ma'am. Everyone is." He swallowed. "I know my running for the Young Miss Homemaker Scholarship is unusual."

"Unusual, Mr. Masterson?" She frowned. "Try bizarre. I've never heard of a *boy* trying for this award. I thought all you fellows lived in front of a television unless, of course, it's time to eat. Then you move to a refrigerator."

"That's just it, Mrs. Bristol, Isabel, ma'am. I'm not like most other boys!"

He paused, reflecting on how the phrase might've sounded, and hastily corrected himself. "I mean, I *am* like most other boys in everything else *but this*. I'm not kidding around, Mrs. Bristol, Isabel, ma'am. This is a serious pursuit for me."

She closed her eyes. "Please, just Mrs. Bristol. Leave off the Isabel, and ma'am."

"Yes, ma'am. Er—should I have said Mrs. Bristol?"

"Forget it."

"Maybe the other boys in your class are there just to chase the girls, but I'm not. I enrolled in home ec for one purpose and one purpose only and that was to learn to be a better homemaker."

He held his breath, waiting.

Mrs. Bristol's lips twitched. "Please go on."

"I've done a lot of meditating about this scholarship, and if I didn't think I could qualify for it, I wouldn't be here asking for the application."

"You sound very sure of yourself, Mr. Masterson."

"Really?"

"Well, actually, no. But you're certainly trying hard enough to impress me."

"That's good, Mrs. Bristol, because I'm very determined to go through with my candidacy."

## The New Man

"And you can guarantee that this isn't a dare or some kind of demented joke?"

"Absolutely. It's one hundred percent sincere."

"All right. Wait a moment. I'll be right back." She left briskly and returned in a few minutes. Handing him several sheets of paper, she said, "Here is your application. Make it as neat as you can. Neatness counts in everything, including your application."

"Thank you, Mrs. Bristol, ma—" He stopped himself. "Well, I guess I'd better be going. I promised your husband I wouldn't keep you too long. I'd really like to thank you for your help in this." Stuffing the papers into the back pocket of his jeans, he turned to leave.

"Rick," he heard her call behind him.

"Yes, ma'am?" He swung around to face her.

"I think you should know that I voted against allowing males to enter the competition."

## Chapter Six

Rick stared grimly at the expensive-looking house. It was twice as large as his own home and possessed a real asphalt driveway. Most of the drives in his neighborhood consisted of dirt, rock or gravel. And none of them had such fancy oak shutters or such costly tile roofs.

"So what are you waiting for?" B.R. asked. "Why don't you get out?"

"It's not that easy. I've never been in there before."

"Oh, come on, Rick. It's just a house."

"No." He pointed to the building beside it. "That's just a house. This immense structure before us is

*Joany's house.* That makes it different from any other place in Redona."

"You'll be fine. Just don't bark at anyone or scratch behind your ear with your foot."

B.R. howled at his own joke until Rick stared him into silence.

"Well, anyway, I don't think you're going to help yourself by getting overly worried," he said.

"Easy for you to say."

"Think of it this way. She wants you in there."

"How do you know that?"

"Because she asked you to come."

"Oh. Yeah."

"Everyone knows you're one of the only kids in school who's pulling an *A* in Mr. Winston's physics class. She's probably going to ask you to help her with some math course."

"You think so?"

"Sure. She said she needed help with her homework. What else are you qualified to assist her with? Meringue?"

"No wisecracks, B.R."

"Wouldn't think of it."

"Well." Rick glanced at his rearview mirror and brushed at his thick blond curls. "I better get going."

"Yeah, you better. It's no fun when you lend me your truck and then don't get out of the driver's seat."

"Okay, okay. Now remember, pick me up at seven-thirty sharp. If she wants me to stay longer, I'll wave to you from the door. Got it?"

"Got it."

"Be careful with my wheels, too."

"I always am."

"And watch out that you don't lug the engine."

"Never."

Rick squared his shoulders. "Well, I guess this is it. Wish me the best, old buddy."

"The best, ole buddy."

He opened the door of his pickup understanding only too well how critical the next two hours of his life were going to be. He'd dreamed of walking into Joany's house a hundred times in the past. It had always been with him carrying something in his hands: flowers, candy, picnic lunches. This time he would be toting a pile of textbooks with him. Not nearly so romantic, but very practical in getting to know a person better.

It was exciting in one sense, having a wish come true. In another way, it was scary. What if things didn't work out the way he'd always assumed they would? What if she didn't like him, or even worse, that he discovered she liked someone else better? What if she thought he was stupid or gross, or told him his breath smelled like a camel's?

Had he brushed his teeth?

Three times, with two different brands of toothpaste.

Anyway, he was sure she wouldn't say anything so crass about someone's personal hygiene. He'd been hanging around B.R. too long. Only guys like him showed such a lack of finesse.

"Well, I'm going now," he remarked with questionable finality, once more.

"Yeah, so I see."

"Okay. We'll see you later."

"Okay. Later."

Rick started across the street, but this time it was B.R. who stopped him. "Uh, there's one more thing, Rick."

"Yeah?"

"Try not to sneeze."

"What?"

"Don't sneeze."

"Why would I do that?"

"Joany's got cats."

*"Cats?"*

"Six of them."

"Six!" He was allergic to cats. Whenever he came within four feet of one, his nose turned red, his eyes swelled and he sneezed. Not just once, but repeatedly, until the cat ran away or someone removed it. "Why didn't you tell me?"

"I didn't want to worry you."

Rick gave a short, hysterical laugh. "So why are you telling me now!"

"To warn you, I guess." B.R. started the truck engine. "You'll do fine, old buddy. I have confidence in you. Just find a room where the cats don't hang out and study there." He pulled from the curb and sped away.

All these years and Rick had never known about Joany's love for felines. Well, it was too late now. He clenched his jaw and started with long determined strides across the street. He would show B.R. a thing or three about true love relationships! When two people really care about each other, nothing as trivial as a half-dozen cats could keep them apart. In such cases adjustments can be made with willingness and poise. Rick could either use an antihistamine or Joany could compromise by switching her affections to parrots, or dogs, or guppies, or something. Or maybe she could simply cut the number of animals down to one, or none, instead of six.

In the meantime he would try not to offend her by sneezing at her pets. Today was too important to ruin with an allergy attack. He simply wouldn't let things end that way.

"Hi, Rick." Joany's brown eyes twinkled with friendliness.

"Hi, Joany." A broad, uncontrollable smile spread across his face.

"Come in. I've been waiting for you."

Rick stepped inside and quickly glanced at the front room and entryway.

"You have a very nice home, Joany," he commented.

"Thank you. Mom had a decorator."

Rick started for the plump couch, but Joany quickly stopped him. "We're not allowed in the parlor except for special occasions," she explained. "We'll study in the den."

She led him through a spotless dining area with a crystal chandelier to the paneled den in the very back of the house.

Rick's nose immediately began to itch. His heartbeat increased with the realization that a sneeze was coming on.

"This is where I usually do my homework. It's much more comfortable in here and most of the time it's quiet." She motioned toward a table and two chairs in the far corner of the room. "I take off the chessboard and work there."

Rick didn't need to actually see the furry bodies to know that at least two cats were intertwined contentedly on each seat.

He counted the seconds with an insurmountable will until Joany turned her head and he could suppress a second sneeze.

"We'll have to move the kitties, too, of course. This is their favorite spot, the little rascals. That's Muffin, Charlie, Puffy, and the white furry one is called Snowball. She drives Mom absolutely crazy with all her long hair. Clara and Paws are outside."

"Snowball." Rick muttered.

"Do you like cats?" she asked.

"Sure, cats are, are, uhh, uhhhh-choo!" He swallowed and blinked. "Nice."

"I love them. They have so much personality."

"Uh-huh. Listen, Joany, perhaps we could study outside today? It's still uh-uhh-uhhh-choo!" He rubbed his mouth. "Warm enough."

"Why that's a wonderful idea! We can sit by the pool in the sun!" She grabbed a pile of books from the sofa and opened the sliding glass door that led to the patio.

Once outside, the tickling sensation left Rick's nose. As long as Snowball and the gang didn't decide to park it on his lap, he would be fine in the open air. He hadn't been in the den long enough to suffer a full-fledged sneezing spell.

Joany led him to an umbrella table with two corduroy lounge chairs and motioned for him to sit. She explained that she'd been having trouble in her geometry class and needed someone to help her work through a few problems. Rick felt a sense of satisfaction knowing he was actually able to help someone as perfect as Joany. He discovered all over again how pretty she was, and several times he nearly lost his concentration being so close to her.

"Would you like to stop for a break?" she asked, after working through their first three problems.

"Sure." He felt like kissing her, but the time wasn't right. At the moment he was the only one thinking of romance. Her mind was probably filled with pyramids, axis and lines.

"Come on. Mom bought a chocolate cake at the bakery last night. I think we have some lemonade, too."

Rick rose to follow her inside, too absorbed with the moment—the fact that he was actually with her, alone, to realize what he was doing. Only after he was leaning against the shiny orange counter in the kitchen and his eyes began to water did he comprehend the severity of his mistake.

He felt something pressing against his leg, and he glanced down, his nostril burning with a tickle. He lifted the cat away with his foot and pushed it with the tip of his sneaker toward the door.

It shoved its rump in the air, stubbornly backing against Rick's attempts to make it move. It finally gave him a long, disgusted stare, sat down and began licking its fur.

"Paws! When did you get back?" Joany exclaimed, poking her head above the refrigerator door. Rick immediately moved his foot away as she rushed over and scooped the large tomcat in her arms.

He felt the nudging around his legs again and discovered that Snowball had come to join them. A meow sounded from the doorway, and Muffin, Charlie and Puffy sauntered in.

"They think I'm going to feed them," she explained.

"Listen, Joany, I'm going to head outside and get the next problem started," Rick said, counting to himself as he held his breath.

"Wait a second, Rick, I want you to meet Paws. Paws has been a bad boy! Gone for two days. Naughty!" She shook her finger at its small black nose.

Paws laid his ears flat.

"Pawsy was my first cat. Oh, we had others, but this baby boy was the first one I could call my own. Right, Pawsy?"

"He's cute. Really Joa-Joa-Jah-choo! I think I should go ahead and wait outside."

"Would you like to hold him?"

"No."

"What?"

"I mean, uhhh-choo! Sure."

She delivered Paws into his hands.

"Nice to meet you, Paws," he said in one breath, before lifting the big ball of fur back to Joany. He felt a huge sneeze coming on as he was holding the cat midair, and he couldn't deposit him in Joany's arms quickly enough. The startled animal spat and scratched Rick's hand as it leaped to the floor.

Before Rick could recover from the first sneeze, another followed. He stepped back and found that Snowball had wound herself between his legs. Unintentionally he pinched one of her paws beneath his tennis shoe, and she let loose a hair-raising yowl, causing all the other cats to duck and freeze with alarm.

"Snowball!" Joany squealed. She reached down for her pet, but as soon as Rick gave the frightened animal enough room, it raced away on three legs.

"I'm, I'm, mmmmmm-choo! Sorry, Joany." Rick gasped for air.

"I think she's hurt!"

"No, I'm sure I only pinched her, er, er, uhh-chooo! paw a little."

"But she cried so loud." Joany ducked his next sneeze, then straightened to glare at him. "What is wrong with you, Rick Masterson!" she demanded.

"I'm really sorry, Joany. I'm aler, aler, uhh-choo!"

"I can't understand you when you keep sneezing that way!" She glanced down the hallway. "It doesn't matter anyway. I have to find Snowball and Paws again. I think they're upset."

"I'll help you, yu, uhhh-choo!"

"No, thanks. Really. I think they're afraid of you. Besides, you should go home and go to bed. Obviously you're coming down with some sort of horrible cold. It isn't considerate to spread germs."

One of the cats slunk through the kitchen, hugging the cabinets in an attempt to be as far from Rick as possible. Joany cooed it's name, but after shooting a wary glance at Rick, it only hurried away faster. It too gave Rick an accusing glare.

While he continued sneezing, Joany left for the patio and collected Rick's books. When she returned she repeated several thank-you's for helping her with her homework and ushered him swiftly to the entryway. "Take something for that cold," she instructed, opening the door.

Rick turned around after he'd stepped outside. "I'm really sorry, Joany. I, er, ahh-ahhh-choo! didn't mean to smash Snowball's paw."

"That's all right. Thanks again. Goodbye."

A few seconds later he was staring into wood.

"Yes, goodbye, Joany," he said softly to himself. He couldn't remember ever feeling so dejected, not even the Day of the Apron could compare with the sinking feeling in his stomach. He'd made himself look like a fool in front of her! A complete jerk! She probably thought of him like an ape in a crystal shop. Clumsy, and dumb, and insensitive.

It wasn't even close to seven-thirty, the time B.R. was due to pick him up. The only way to leave the area was by foot. He rearranged his books and walked away. He wanted to put as much distance as he could between Joany's home and himself.

It was dark by the time he reached Main Street, yet he felt himself drawn toward the turnoff to the Humpty Dump-All Nursery School. By the time he'd walked approximately four miles to get there the front porch steps looked as inviting to him as an easy chair.

He sat down and leaned his back against the door.

## Chapter Seven

Rick had hoped by studying with Joany he might find the courage to tell her about his candidacy for the Young Miss Homemaker Scholarship. That was only a pathetic dream now. After what had happened that day, he knew that perfect moment to explain had passed. He toyed with the idea of withdrawing from the competition. It seemed the only way left to remain friends with Joany.

"What have I done?" he moaned aloud, sinking his head between his folded arms.

"I don't know, Rick. What have you done?"

He nearly jumped at the unexpected voice. Looking up, he recognized Heidi's pretty oval face outlined by moonlight.

His lips curved into a weak grin. "You almost gave me a heart attack."

"Sorry. I thought you heard me drive up."

"I guess I was concentrating on something else."

"And I'll bet it wasn't concerts, fairs or circuses." She searched his troubled face. "You look as though you just lost your best friend."

He forced an awkward laugh. "That good, eh? It's just been one of those days."

"May I sit down?" she asked.

"Sure."

She sank down beside him. "How long have you been here?"

"I dunno. I guess I haven't checked my watch yet. What time do you have?"

"Eight-thirty."

"Eight-thirty!" He glanced at his wrist as if it was too outrageous to believe.

"Rick," Heidi said.

"Yes."

She found his somber gaze and held it locked for a few minutes, gently communicating her concern without words. "What's wrong?"

"Oh, I dunno, Heidi. It's just a bunch of stuff."

"What stuff?"

"Oh, I dunno."

To his surprise, he felt her fingers wrap around his hand.

"I know you have a problem, Rick, and I'd really like to help."

"All right," he finally conceded. "I'm having trouble with this friend," he began.

"Guy or girl?"

"Girl."

Heidi nodded, encouraging him to go on.

"You see, I've been trying to get to know her better for years. Centuries. And tonight, miracle of miracles, she asked me over to her house, and..." He stopped, too grieved by the memory to continue.

"Go ahead, Rick. And what?"

He sighed. "And I blew it. Ruined everything beyond repair."

"I don't believe you. You're not the type to mess up like that."

"It's true. I offended her and ruined the peace of her home."

"How?" Her voice was more than a little skeptical.

"I sneezed at all of her cats."

"Excuse me?"

"Her cats. I sneezed at them. I tripped over one, too, and pinched its paw so that it yowled."

"Was it okay?"

"Yeah, but I'm sure its toes are a little sore."

"I don't think I understand, Rick. Try to explain it better."

"My friend?"

"Yes."

"She has cats."

"Uh-huh."

"Six of them."

"So?"

"And I'm allergic to them. Not just a few sniffles allergic, but real blow-the-house-down-with-sneezes allergic. I get around that fluffy hair and I can't control myself."

"Rick," Heidi interrupted. "That's not your fault. It's an allergy. She can't hold that against you."

"Maybe, but I think she does." He groaned. "I mean, she looked so mad. And she asked me to leave because I was upsetting the cats so much."

"That doesn't mean she blames you. She probably just meant that it was better if you were gone so she could get things under control again. I'm sure her feelings for you aren't going to change simply because you're allergic to cats." She became quiet for a few seconds. "I know mine wouldn't."

"Okay, shoot." She folded her arms over her knees so that the two of them were in matched positions.

"I know something that she doesn't know, and when she finds out I think she's going to be even more angry."

"I can't believe it! What is it you know?"

"That we're competing for the same college scholarship."

Heidi stared at him, a perplexed expression forming a frown on her normally smooth forehead. "Forgive me, Rick, but I'm afraid I don't understand again. I mean, the crime just doesn't seem that serious."

"Well, if you knew what scholarship it was, I think you'd understand."

"Okay. What scholarship is it?"

Rick felt the usual lump of clay attach itself to his vocal chords. He guessed the words would never come easy for him, no matter how often he said them.

"Is it an academic scholarship?" she questioned coaxingly.

"Not really."

"It isn't an athletic one, is it?"

He paused, took a long quivering breath and then met her gaze evenly. "You promise not to laugh or anything?"

"Okay. All right."

"Now you might—think it's funny, so you have to be sure."

"I am. How hilarious could a scholarship be?"

He squared his shoulders. "Okay. We're both competing for the Young Miss Homemaker Scholarship."

His words came out so rushed that Heidi asked him to repeat them.

"I said, Joany and I are both competing for the Young Miss Homemaker Scholarship."

At first Heidi didn't answer, but Rick was positive the corners of her mouth were twitching.

"You promised," he said reproachfully.

"Who's laughing? Go on!"

"The scholarship is for two thousand dollars," he said doggedly.

"Wow! That's more than any of the scholarships at our school."

"You've got it. It's the only chance I have for getting a degree in computer programming and analysis.

And the sponsors didn't stipulate that the recipient of the award had to be female."

"I see," she said.

"You do?" Rick's expression brightened.

"Of course. And you know, Rick, if I can see the logic in you trying for the scholarship, I'll bet your friend will, too. She shouldn't act any differently toward you than she would if the two of you were competing for an athletic award."

Heidi sounded so sure that Rick began to wonder if she could be right. Maybe he'd been looking at his predicament from the wrong perspective. After all, he had committed no crime—he had as much right as anyone to compete for the award.

"I'm sorry, Rick," Heidi interrupted his thoughts. "As much as I'd like to stay and talk longer, I have to go. Clara was afraid that one of the girls forgot to lock the front door, so she asked me to drive down and check it. She couldn't do it herself because her husband had the car." She stood, grabbed the doorknob and jiggled it. "Wouldn't you know? Locked." She glanced down at Rick and smiled. "I'm glad I drove over anyway."

He scrambled to his feet. "I'm glad you came, too. Not only because you made me feel tons better..." He hesitated and grinned sheepishly. "But also because I need a ride."

She laughed. "It's usually the other way around. You always come in at just the right second to save Clara and me from some horrendous disaster. It's nice being able to return the favor."

"I think you've evened the score tonight, Heidi," he said.

Mrs. Bristol surveyed the room of mournful-looking students, her dissatisfaction as evident as a police sergeant who had uncovered a restaurant of sleeping cops.

Wolf slunk farther into his chair. Rick's eyebrows furrowed close with concern. Two girls whispered nervously.

"This test wasn't any different from the others. You knew when it was coming. All the necessary information was given during class lectures. And—" her expression grew even more sardonic "—there's always our textbook. Some of you could've tried opening it."

Wolf let out a laugh. Her razor-sharp look silenced him.

"Sixty percent of the class failed or were below average. Thirty percent barely pulled a *C*. Only one person managed a *B*, and there was a grand total of two *A*'s out of thirty alive, and supposedly thinking human beings." She took a deep breath while the class waited in wary sullenness.

"I see no other alternative but to have you people take the entire test over again, excluding the three persons who received the above-average marks. Anyone who pulls less than a *B* on this second exam will need to do makeup work to justify it." Ignoring student groans she continued, "Need I remind everyone that this is not a mind-busting course? There are no logbooks, formulas or periodical charts to memorize. No one is under pressure to learn the secret of humanoid cloning or what's in the core of the great planet Earth.

"If anyone feels that pulling an acceptable grade on the next test is beyond her capabilities, she may ask those three who so magnificently managed the miracle of answering twelve simple questions in a row correctly. Their names are listed on the bulletin board beside the door. I'm withholding the test papers until after the makeup exam. Class dismissed!"

There was a jam of bodies at the doorway as everyone slowed to see who had passed the test. Although Mrs. Bristol acted as though the quiz was the same as all the others, it had actually required more preparation and study. Rick had estimated that it would be more difficult than past tests and had spent an additional hour studying for it.

It paid off, too. As he neared the door, he was greatly relieved to see his name was printed second on the list.

Joany Rhoads, naturally, was first.

He glanced over his shoulder and spotted her behind him. As usual, Wolf was beside her, so Rick decided he wouldn't drop back to congratulate her. Instead he gave her the thumbs-up signal, and she returned a friendly smile.

It had been one month since the Day of the Cats.

And, as Rick had feared, it had taken him longer to make up for his second error. He had needed energy and diligence to convince Joany that he liked her pets.

## The New Man

Heidi had been correct on that point. Joany hadn't blamed him for what had happened because of his sneezing, and Rick was feeling more confident that Heidi was right about her being able to accept his candidacy for the scholarship, as well.

As yet he'd still not gathered enough courage to tell her. It wasn't all pure cowardice, either. The opportunities to talk to her alone were dwindling. For one thing Wolf was always around like gum on her shoe. And whenever she did manage to shake him long enough to find Rick, there was always some appointment he had to keep.

He never seemed to have the time to initiate an in-depth conversation. He'd increased his volunteer hours at Humpty Dump-All Nursery School to include Wednesdays, and Heidi had convinced him to enroll in a six-week sewing course sponsored by the Junior College every Thursday night. Combined with his usual weekend yard jobs, meetings and homework, he scarcely had a moment to himself.

He wasn't complaining. Rick really enjoyed his work at the nursery school. The kids, although trying, were fun to be around and proved to be a great source of personal satisfaction.

Another advantage of his volunteer work was his continued companionship with Heidi. She'd become a trusted friend and could always be depended upon for advice and encouragement. Even B.R. had approved of Heidi. He said if he'd known she was working at the nursery school, he would have volunteered, too.

Rick found that he was always in his best moods when he knew he would be inhaling Play-Doh after school.

Like today. He was humming in the halls, completely unaffected by the din around him. It took B.R. three calls and a pencil poke in the rump to finally catch his attention.

"Hey!" Rick growled. "Watch it!"

"What are you, deaf or something?"

"I tune myself out to unimportant noises."

"Well, thanks a lot. I'm here for your benefit, buddy, not mine."

"Oh, yeah? What's up? Got a check for a million dollars to deliver?"

"No. I've come as your personal agent. I'm making sure you did everything you were supposed to today."

"Okay, let's see. I took a shower, shaved, brushed my teeth, located clean socks, kissed my mom goodbye—"

"Don't be moronic." B.R.'s eyes narrowed as he glanced warily down both directions of the hall. He lowered his voice. "You know. Did you do what you were supposed to do with the papers. T-h-e p-a-p-e-r-s."

"Ohh." Rick nodded and motioned B.R. to follow him to his locker. He began twirling the combination lock and kept his tone as hushed as B.R.'s. "I handed the application to Mrs. Bristol this morning. I snuck into her class early, before anyone else was around."

"Did she agree to keep it secret?"

"Not secret. Confidential. I told her there were some people who might take offense at my candidacy and that I needed the time to break the news to them diplomatically."

"She didn't think that was weird?"

"Are you kidding? She thinks everything I do is weird." He deposited two books into his locker and pulled three more out. "But at least she isn't so negative about it anymore. She's giving me the opportunity to try for it."

"Did you include the sewing part?"

Rick stifled B.R. with his hand. "Keep it down, will you?"

"Sorry." Checking for eavesdroppers, he extended his thin neck until his Adam's apple looked like a golf ball. "I just wanted to make sure that you put all your positive points down. Sewing is a praiseworthy credit to a homemaker."

"Yes, yes I know. A real penny saver. A couple weeks from now and I should be completing my first skirt."

"Skirt?" B.R. busted out in a loud guffaw. "Is it one with a split up the front? Or just a ruffle around the bottom?"

"Funny." Rick closed the locker with a denting 'bang' from his elbow. "I didn't know we could make anything else until I'd already cut the pattern out. The instructor keeps forgetting there's a guy in the class. When she finally remembered to tell me I could exchange the skirt for a shirt, it was too late. Anyway, a skirt is about five million times easier to make than a shirt."

"Hi, Rick," a girl said, cutting between them.

"Hi, Michelle," he returned without losing his train of thought.

B.R. pivoted on his heels and walked backward to watch the pretty brunette. "You sure are getting to know a lot of girls," he commented.

"Comes with the territory, I guess."

"What are you going to do with a skirt?"

"If it turns out decent enough, I'd like to give it to Heidi."

"Heidi?" B.R. faked a look of astonishment. "What about the love-of-your-life, Joany? Are my ears deceiving me or are you falling for another woman?"

"Don't act spastic," Rick said crossly. "It draws attention from teachers."

"I can't help it. I'm in shock."

"I would give it to Joany, but I'm not sure she'd like it. I thought Heidi would be a better choice since she's the one who convinced me that I could handle the sewing course in the first place."

B.R. whistled. "I give credit where credit's due! You're doing a great job! In the beginning I wasn't so sure you could handle things. You know, the pressure, all the new stuff you had to learn. A lot of guys would've cracked. But you're still hanging in there."

"Yeah, well, I want to do more than just 'hang in there.' What do you think my chances are of actually winning the scholarship?"

"You want the truth?"

"Nothing but or I'll use your head for a pastry pan."

"I'd say they're good. In fact I can't think of many other people who are involved in as much as you are and have still been able to maintain a decent grade average."

"Excluding sports?"

"Excluding sports. In my opinion there's only one person who's really qualified to give you a run for your money."

Rick nodded. It was as clear as the tardy bell drilling through the halls like a broken foghorn. His strongest competitor for the Young Miss Homemaker Scholarship was Joany Rhoads.

## Chapter Eight

Beany!" Heidi's voice echoed through the cluttered room, drawing everyone's attention to the dark-haired boy in the corner. At the same instant she noticed Rick's tall figure silhouetted in the doorway. "Could you get him, Rick?" she called. "He's pasting flash cards on the wall with peanut butter!"

"No problem." He leaped several Tonka trucks, zigzagged between desks and slid past several toddlers to Beany who was intently smearing smashed peanuts on the backs of word cards with his fingers. Several pieces of paper were already fixed firmly on the wall, along with a dangling crayon and a building block.

"Hands out, Beany!" Rick commanded, standing clear of the gooey substances surrounding him. "Your glue career is over! March to the bathroom, locate a bar of soap and start scrubbing!"

Rick winked at Heidi as they tromped by. She giggled before she returned to her nursing duties of stretching a Band-Aid over a youngster's wounded knee cap.

"Two of the kids needed a ride home, and Clara had to take them," Heidi explained later as she and Rick stooped to their knees and busied themselves cleaning the sticky wall. "Whenever Beany notices the troops are down, he plans an attack."

"He doesn't play very fair, does he?"

"That's putting it mildly."

"When you've finished that mess, I brought a present for you," Rick announced abruptly, wiping the last brown clump with his sponge.

"For me?" Heidi's eyes sparkled with pleasure. "What for?"

"For being such a nice girl." He took her hand and helped her to her feet. "And for being such a good friend."

To Rick's surprise, her smooth olive-toned skin turned a shade darker and her gaze fell from his.

"Here, I'll get it for you." He went to the cabinet, where he'd stuffed the brown-paper sack, and hurried back. "I would have wrapped it, but my wrapping's not that great."

"That's okay." She smiled shyly and he handed her the package.

"Go ahead. Open it. The kids will be done with their graham crackers soon, and we might not get another chance."

She gave a quick nod, then unfolded the sack and peeked inside. Glancing bewilderedly at Rick, she pulled the corduroy skirt into full view. It was a light-wine color with a tailored slit in the front.

"It's really pretty, Rick!" she exclaimed.

He couldn't get the words, "Thanks, I made it myself," to leave his mouth, so he just said, "I'm glad you like it."

He was aware that a large percentage of fashion designers around the world were male. Nevertheless, he didn't feel comfortable admitting that he'd made the skirt and was grateful that Heidi was too polite to ask where he'd bought it.

"Do you think it'll fit?" Rick watched as she held the skirt to her waist. Silently he congratulated himself.

He'd figured her size perfectly.

"It looks perfect. Thank you so much!" She stretched to the tip of her toes and kissed him.

His breath quickened as he found himself wanting to pull her closer and kiss her back.

Cad, he scolded himself. Untrustworthy philanderer! He'd known Joany almost forever, and there was never any doubt in his heart that she was the only girl for him. Sitting beside Wolf for an hour every day, listening to his sleazy remarks about women, had finally gotten to him. Wolf had infiltrated Rick's mind so he was actually beginning to think like him!

"Clara's back," Heidi announced, calling Rick back to reality.

"Oh. Yes. I see. I'll start picking up the kids' napkins and cups." He started away but Heidi caught his arm.

"Don't worry about it. We can get them in a second." She gestured for him to follow her to one of the back tables. Lifting herself to sit on top, she patted the surface next to her, indicating that she wanted him to follow suit. "I thought we could take a few minutes to talk."

"Okay."

"It's about the scholarship," she began. "I was wondering how things were going."

"Pretty good, I think."

"And home ec?"

"I'm pulling an *A* average in all my classes this year, so the whole academic thing looks impressive, honor roll even. My only worry is Mrs. Bristol. I killed another batch of brownies last week, and my creamed toast wouldn't stop moving on the plate."

"What's all that have to do with Mrs. Bristol?"

"I don't know. I get the feeling she doesn't appreciate people messing up on meals or males trying for awards that were meant for females."

"But she did agree to give you the application, remember?"

"Sure, but that doesn't mean she'll actually allow me to win the scholarship."

"I bet she will if you continue to prove to her that you're a qualified candidate."

"I hope you're right."

"Well, what does Joany think? Does she say Mrs. Bristol will judge you unfairly?"

"We better get back to the kids. It'll be time for cleanup soon," he said evasively.

"Really, Rick. It's okay. We'll just be a few more minutes. So what about Joany? What's her opinion?"

He held back the reply. "Ready to get busy? Cups are all over the place."

"You haven't told her yet, have you? She still doesn't know, does she?"

"I haven't been able to find the right moment," he admitted.

"But, Rick, it's been six weeks since we first talked about it! Every Friday I ask you about it, and every Friday you promise you're going to take care of it. Don't you see? The longer you wait the worse it's going to be."

"Yes, but..." Rick threw his hands up helplessly. "You don't know how easy it is to get her upset. I need to tell her in exactly the right way. And there never seems to be enough time."

Heidi eyed him skeptically. "Well, now you're really going to find time."

"What do you mean?"

"They're going to start the interviews in two weeks."

"How do you know?"

"I have an inside connection."

"Who?"

Heidi glanced across the noisy room at Clara as she dumped her second load of paper cups into the trash.

"When did you find out?"

"Yesterday. We were talking about all the different clubs in town and the Young Miss Homemaker Scholarship naturally came up. She's been a member of the Redona Society of American Homemakers for over two years now. I just never knew it."

"Two weeks," Rick murmured to himself. "The grades, Humpty Dump-All, home ec, the extra night courses. It all comes together in two weeks."

"That's right," Heidi confirmed, folding her arms across her chest. "Which means only two more Mondays left to tell Joany before she *finds it out herself.*"

## Chapter Nine

Rick pivoted on his heel and dribbled the basketball at a dead run toward the end of the court.

B.R. was breathing heavily behind him. At the last second he made one gallant, three-foot leap in a vain attempt to stop Rick's arrow-sharp shot.

They collided midair and fell backward, their legs entangled like strands of spaghetti.

"Playing with you is almost as safe as playing with a drunken rhinoceros," Rick wheezed, untangling himself to stand.

"Yeah, well, it's not exactly a picnic with you, either. I need some sort of handicap to make the game fair."

Rick jogged after the ball and leisurely bounced it back. He hadn't been able to play a decent game of basketball at the park for weeks. It felt great to be holding a basketball in his hands. "I gave you a ten-point lead, Bones old man. If you can't handle the fire, then drop the hose."

B.R. tiredly drew himself to his feet. "I need at least a twenty-point spot to feel even a twinge of inspiration."

Rick sent the ball sailing through the hoop. "There's only thirty-six points to a game. Why don't I just call you the winner before we start?"

"What about me? I can help even things up."

B.R. turned around. Rick silenced the ball against his stomach. They surveyed the new arrival to the court with cynicism.

"Sure, Wolf," Rick said. "Me against you and Bones. No leads. My ball first."

He could tell B.R. wasn't exactly thrilled to have Wolf added to the game, but he nodded in agreement anyway. It was unusual for Wolf to even ask to play. It wasn't his style. There were too many car stereos and hub caps left unattended at that time of the day for him to waste his energy on sports.

Rick immediately jumped to a four-point lead and quickly discovered that Wolf was as honest about playing basketball as he was at earning an income.

Either that or the poor guy was clumsy. He was always smashing against Rick, jabbing him with an elbow or tripping into him. A few times Rick felt the anger burst within him. He'd swing around, his jaw clenched tightly, ready to face Wolf at the final showdown, but Wolf, puffing and wheezing, was always busy at something else, scrambling after the ball, stumbling over B.R., dribbling in the wrong direction...

He appeared to be such a genuine klutz, Rick found it was hardly worth the effort of a confrontation.

At last, after many bruises, skidding falls and collisions, the game ended 36-32, in Rick's favor.

To his surprise, Wolf tripped over and slapped him five, weakly.

"Good game, guy," he coughed, seemingly unable to stop.

"Thanks." Rick exchanged glances with B.R. "Are you okay?"

"Sure," he hacked. "I'm just not used to doing this sort of thing."

"What made you decide to change your life today?" B.R. questioned, tucking the ball against his side as he and Rick hooked arms with Wolf to help him to his car.

"I wasn't planning to, but I needed to talk to my partner here. His mom told me I could find him at the park."

They half dragged Wolf the last few steps to the street, and he collapsed against the hood of his car. "Oh, man, was that fun," he wheezed, laying his hot, flushed cheek against the cool black paint.

"Glad you had a good time." Rick grinned at B.R. "I've got a meeting to make tonight, Wolf, so if you have something you want to talk to me about, better get started."

"It's about my Joany-Oany," he said.

Rick felt the back of his neck prickle. "What about her?"

"I just wanted to let you know I'm going to ask her to the banquet with me, and I don't want any hard feelings."

"What banquet?" He stepped closer.

"You know, that woman's banquet. The American Housemakers or something or other. The doll's club in town."

"You mean The Redona Society of American Homemakers?" B.R. asked in a menacing voice.

"Yeah, yeah. Them. Joany's trying for their scholarship, and all the candidates are going to be invited to go. I plan to volunteer myself to escort Joany." He noticed Rick's glowering stare. "Now, now, partner. I know you wouldn't hit a man when he's down. I can hardly stand, let alone defend myself."

"When did you hear about the banquet?" Rick demanded.

"Today. After the quiz. Didn't you catch Mrs. Bristol's announcement?"

"No." After the quiz all his attention had been focused on Joany. "When is it?"

"In a couple of weeks. On a Friday. Seven o—hey!" His eyes narrowed. "You're asking all these questions so you can get to Joany first! You're planning to offer yourself as an escort before I get the chance to."

Actually the thought hadn't occurred to Rick. But now that Wolf had mentioned it...

The two boys glared at each other.

B.R. shuffled nervously, glancing from one to the other. The seconds ticked slowly by.

Suddenly Wolf bolted toward his car door.

In the same half second Rick leaped from the street into a dead run toward his truck across the park. His muscles working double-time, he ran at such a great speed that B.R. was left yelling helplessly after him.

"Wait by the street!" Rick shouted without wasting any strength to look back. "I'll swing by."

Jerking his truck door open, he jumped inside, cranked it up and shoved it in first gear. He reached over and pushed the passenger's door ajar as he approached B.R. Slowing, but never bringing the truck to a complete stop, B.R. was forced to run alongside until he could grab on to the handle and throw himself into the seat.

"Risking life and limb for a stupid girl!" he shouted, trying to pull the door shut before Rick increased his speed any further.

"She's not stupid!" Rick yelled back.

He had to reach his house within the next three minutes to make it on time. Wolf lived much farther away, and Rick was guessing he'd stop at the gas station two blocks down Main Street, rather than risk driving all the way to his house.

"You're never going to make it," B.R. said. "Why don't you just give up and ask Heidi to go with you?"

## The New Man

The tires squealed as Rick took a sharp corner. "I have to ask Joany," he said. "All the years I've known her, and she's never so much as given a second glance in my direction. This semester she's finally recognized that I'm alive. I think now that the apron and cat thing are over with, she might even start liking me." He glanced at B.R. and nearly missed the second corner, braking to get control of the truck again.

B.R. yelped and covered his eyes. "It sounds like you're going to ask her to go with you for all the past years that she ignored you, not because you like her now."

The tires screamed to a halt as Rick pulled into his driveway.

"Don't bother me with unimportant details!" he barked, nearly tripping as he scrambled from the truck and raced toward the house.

"Unimportant details?" B.R. yelled after him. "Facts!" He fell back against the seat as he watched his best friend slam the door behind him. "When will that guy learn?" he mumbled to himself. "Joany's simply not the girl for him...."

Rick let out a window-shattering roar as the busy signal sounded in his ear. If his mother had been home, she would've had puppies. There was a note on the desk beside the phone.

Rick,
I ran to the store. Be back in twenty minutes. A boy named Wolf? stopped by to speak with you.

Did his parents really name him that?

                                            Love, Mom

He picked up the receiver and dialed Joany's number again. Maybe Joany hadn't been talking to Wolf. Maybe one of her girl friends had called her, or perhaps Mr. or Mrs. Rhoads had decided to use the phone for a few minutes.

The busy signal blared in his ear again.

He pushed the receiver button down and redialed the number. This time it rang, and his heart leaped to his throat.

What was he going to say? A click sounded and his stomach flopped.

"Hello?"

"Hel, hel. Uh, hi."

"Rick? Is that you?"

"Yes, uh, this is Rick. I tried to call you a minute ago, but the phone was busy."

"Yes, I know. I think it was an obscene call. I answered the phone and this person just kept wheezing and coughing into the receiver. He'd try to talk every few seconds, but there were horns honking and other traffic sounds in the background, and I couldn't tell what he was trying to say. Finally I asked myself what I was doing listening to a fool like that, so I hung up on him."

"You did the right thing," Rick assured her, imagining how Wolf must've felt hearing that abrupt click after rushing to get through to Joany first.

"Actually he sounded kind of familiar."

"Really?"

"We used to have this pug dog with breathing problems. In a way, the noises reminded me of him."

Rick tried not to laugh.

"Puggy died a long time ago, though. He ate a spoiled turkey."

"That's too bad."

"He shouldn't have gotten into the trash."

"I guess not."

"Did you call for a reason, Rick?"

He hastily cleared his throat. "Uh, yes. I did."

"What was it?"

"It's about the banquet that Mrs. Bristol mentioned today."

"Yes?"

"I was wondering if I could take you." Rick's eyes squinted shut as he waited for her answer. A rejection always came better in darkness.

"I think that would be okay. Only... at the risk of sounding conceited, I think you should know that I'll probably be going on stage."

Rick swallowed. His excitement over her acceptance was suddenly replaced by the old familiar anxiety of his secret.

"It's important to look good, if you know what I mean."

"Sure. I understand."

"Do you have a suit?"

"Yes."

"Three-piece?"

"I can find a middle part if you'd like."

"Well, if it's not too much trouble. It's just that they'll be taking pictures of me, and that sort of thing. It'll be to your benefit, too, if you dress in a three-piece."

"If that's what you want, Joany, I'll be happy to oblige."

"Thank you, Rick."

"Anytime, Joany."

## Chapter Ten

The mirror reflected a handsome boy. Alert eyes, strong, square jaw, golden curls.

However, it wasn't the impression Rick received. In frustration he pulled at his tie, tugged the knot loose, and then attacked it again.

"Come on, Rick. Leave it alone." Heidi laughed. "The last three times you redid it, it was perfect."

"Are you sure? I'm positive it was off some. A tie one-tenth of an inch to the side can make a guy's entire body look crooked."

"Well, yours doesn't. Come on, let's go."

"Not my son!" Mrs. Masterson said proudly as Rick walked into the living room to pass her maternal inspection. "You look very handsome, Rick."

"Hear! Hear!" Heidi agreed enthusiastically. "If those judges don't recognize a winner when they see him, then it'll be their own loss. Right, Mrs. Masterson?"

"Absolutely. There's not a better Miss Homemaker in the entire county!"

In spite of his nervousness, Rick laughed. "Thanks, Mom, but I know you're biased."

"I'm not." Heidi stepped over and helped him situate his tie one last time. "You've got an excellent chance of winning. Try to remember that during the interview. And for heaven's sake, relax! You've practiced and prepared, so you can afford to be yourself."

"Not too much like yourself," Mrs. Masterson interjected. "Don't put your feet on their table, or chew gum, or—"

"Don't worry, Mom," he interrupted, leaning down to kiss her on the cheek. He took a deep breath. "I'd better go."

Heidi helped him into his coat and smiled approvingly as he turned to face her. "Knock 'em dead, Captain Rick."

"Thanks, Heidi."

She smiled at him before placing her hands gently on his arms, to pull herself high enough to kiss him. "That's for luck," she said.

Rick floated to his truck. He waved to Heidi and his mom once more before he started the engine. This wasn't the time to try to sort out the mixed emotions that were reeling like a cement mixer inside him. Be-

## The New Man

sides the appointment for his interview for the Young Miss Homemaker Scholarship at the school cafeteria in forty-five minutes, he had made a date to talk with Joany about his candidacy. He wouldn't allow anything to deter his thoughts from what he knew he had to do.

He had no choice. He couldn't put if off even an hour longer. If someone saw him entering or leaving the cafeteria, they might be able to figure out what was going on. Especially any of the girls who were in his home-ec class. Joany's appointment for her interview was a safe three days away from his own, but there were too many other people involved to take the risk. It was incredible that he'd made it this far without anyone suspecting him. To think he could continue any further without being discovered was suicidal.

He stood on Joany's porch several seconds before he forced his finger to the doorbell. He planned to speak to her right where he was because of Snowball, Muffin, Paws, Puffy and the rest of her furry family. Confessing his guilt would be difficult enough without being constantly interrupted with sneezes.

His anxiety intensified as he waited for someone to answer. After he was sure the proper amount of time had passed, he rang the bell again.

Nothing happened. Rick checked his watch to make sure he'd gotten the times straight.

He pressed the button once more.

Oddly, he thought he heard someone shouting his name. It was such a faint sound, it could just as easily have been his imagination. He stepped from the porch, wondering if the noise had come from someplace else.

It sounded again, clearer.

There was no doubt in his mind this time; Joany was calling him. He bolted around the side of the house and met with a six-foot block fence. Her third cry was even more desperate, and he swiftly scaled the wall, dropping with a heavy thud on the opposite side.

He zigzagged through the lounge chairs and umbrella tables until he finally spotted her on her knees on the peach-colored flagstones, now stained with uneven patches of maroon.

"Oh, Rick!" she cried. "I'm glad you heard me! Please help, something horrible has happened!"

Rushing to her side, Rick dropped down, ready to administer all the first aid he knew.

"Where does it hurt, Joany?" he whispered, barely able to speak.

"Not me!" she snapped. "It's Paws. He's been in some sort of awful fight!"

Rick surveyed the bloodstains. "Where is he?"

Slowly she lifted the corner of a towel from across her lap. Angry yellow eyes stared up at Rick.

"Where is he hurt?"

"I'm not sure. All I can find so far is his ear." She pointed to his left side. The skin was torn halfway down the ear to its head.

"Here—" Rick reached over and pulled the rest of the towel back "—let me check to see if I can find anything else." Quickly rolling his coat sleeve up, he began examining the cat with one hand while suppressing sneezes with his other. The big tom tensed, and Joany held him more securely on her lap.

"Have you seen him walk yet?" he asked, standing back several feet for fresh air.

"Yes. I had to chase him around the yard twice to catch him."

"Good. Then nothing's broken. I can't find any other cuts on him. I guess most of the blood is from that ear."

To Rick's immense discomfort, Joany began to cry. "Thank goodness!" she sniffed between wails. "Thank goodness he's going to live!"

He wanted to console her, but he knew if he stepped even one inch closer his nose would burn with sneezes, and it would make Paws try to jump from her lap.

"Please, Rick, you have to help me take him to our veterinarian. Mom and Dad aren't home, and I have no other way go get there!" She covered the injured cat with the towel again.

Rick glanced at his watch. Only twenty minutes remained before his interview. Maybe they woudln't mind if he arrived a few minutes late. He was sure the judges would understand if he explained the circumstances to them.

"Okay," he said, helping Joany to stand. "You carry Paws because I'll only scare him. Is he afraid of riding in cars?"

"No," she managed between wails. "We take our cats driving with us whenever we get the chance."

He made a quick mental note never to ride in the Rhoads's car. "I'm going to sneeze some when we get into the cab, so you'll have to keep a tight hold on him."

"Can you just not sneeze this once?" she protested. "I don't want to frighten my baby anymore than he already is."

"Sorry, Joany. If I could, I would."

She was unable to pull herself to the cab while clutching Paws, so Rick lifted her gently into the passenger's seat. As soon as both doors were securely closed, he succumbed to the ultimate allergy attack.

By the time they pulled into the parking lot, Rick could barely see through his puffy eyes. His nose looked like a clown's, and his face was blotchy and swollen.

He stumbled out of the cab, sucking in as much fresh air as he could. "There," he breathed, holding the door to the veterinarian's office ajar for Joany. "Will you be okay now?"

"What do you mean?" she cried, her eyes beginning to fill with tears again. "You're not thinking of leaving me at a time like this are you?"

"I'm afraid I have no choice, Joany. I have an appointment."

"But I can't do it alone! I'll never be able to handle it!" The first of a series of sobs escaped her trembling lips.

"You don't have anything to worry about, Joany. The doctor will take care of everything for you."

"Pleeeze, Rick. Nothing could be more important than Paws!"

"Okay," he surrendered. "I'll have to leave as soon as the doctor gives his diagnosis though. Okay?"

Joany nodded, and the two of them hurried into the veterinarian's office.


"What cat?" Mrs. Bristol asked, puzzled.

"A friend's cat. It was bleeding all over the place, and I didn't have a choice." Rick pointed to a brown spot on his right coat sleeve. "See, there's some cat blood right there."

"Ugh." Mrs. Bristol closed her eyes. "No need for graphic detail, Mr. Masterson."

"Sorry," he mumbled weakly.

"Why didn't you call?"

"There wasn't time. It was an emergency."

She looked at him in astonishment. "What's the matter with your face?"

"I'm allergic to cats."

"I see. Well, I can't help that. Why did you come?"

Rick squared his broad shoulders and cleared his throat, "I came here to ask for another chance to be interviewed."

"That's impossible." Mrs. Bristol's lips thinned. "The other judges have already left. The only reason I'm still here is because I needed to tally the scores of those candidates who managed to follow through with their interview appointments."

"Is there a possibility I could reschedule?" Rick had resolved to be calm, yet he couldn't keep the desperation from slipping into his voice.

Mrs. Bristol carefully stacked the papers she'd been evaluating and placed them neatly in her notebook. Drawing herself to an erect stand, she looked at him sternly. "Very well, young man," she finally said. "Because of your fine record, I'm going to allow your interview to be rescheduled."

Whether it was the accumulation of all the tensions of the day—the preinterview jitters, Heidi's kiss, Paws, Joany—the strained conversation now or a simple act of madness, when Mrs. Bristol said, "Well, we'll meet here the same time tomorrow for your makeup interview," Rick spontaneously grabbed her. Not for a little chipmunk squeeze, either. But rather, an authentic, shoulder-crushing hippo-hug.

"Mr. Masterson," she protested, struggling to break free. "I'm not against displays of affection, but please."

"I'm sorry, Mrs. Bristol. Really. I guess I just sort of—"

"It's quite all right." She dismissed the embarrassing ordeal with a quick wave of her hand. "Remember this, though, there will be no excuse for missing your appointment a second time, I don't care how many ears this fellow, Paws, cuts. Do I make myself clear young man?"

"Yes, ma'am. Completely." He hurried to the door to open it for her. "Good day, Mrs. Bristol."

She glanced over her shoulder at his splotchy face, basketball nose and dirtied suit. "If you really think so, Mr. Masterson," she replied, a faint hint of amusement curving the corners of her mouth.

## Chapter Eleven

Rick sat on the faded couch, staring at his front door. His dress shirt was neatly creased from the shoulders to the cuffs, his tie was perfectly fixed in place and his socks were fresh from Mel's Department Store. The only items missing from his immaculate attire were his pants and suit coat.

He continued to examine each sliver of wood on the ancient oak door. There was still an hour left before the interview. Rick had made sure every portion of the afternoon was so absolutely systemized that nothing could go wrong. Aside from earthquakes, tornados and other natural disasters, he had covered all fronts.

A knock sounded. He rose, walked across the carpet and opened the door.

## The New Man

"Sorry I'm late!" B.R. rushed into the room and began tugging at the layer of plastic that covered Rick's freshly cleaned suit. "I lost the stupid tag and had to promise on George Washington's grave that you really gave me permission to pick this up. I got tired of waiting and bought a candy bar and now my fingers are sticky. Look, I'm going to get smudges all over it!"

Rick raised a hand. "Bones, my son," he began complacently. "Today there's going to be no such words as 'smudges' or 'late.'"

Sedately he took the plastic-covered hanger from B.R. and began to unwrap the suit.

"Right."

Disregarding B.R.'s bewildered stare, Rick carefully put on the rest of his outfit and stepped to the mirror. Each minor detail was impeccably complete. His hair, teeth, clothes, shoes, everything. He was the perfect specimen of a candidate. He could've walked before a panel of judges anywhere and drawn grand scores for appearance alone.

"What can I do now?" B.R. asked, impressed with Rick's mastery of the situation.

"Your further duties consist of accompanying me from this moment on, until my interview is under way," Rick replied. He pushed his wallet in one pocket and slipped his keys into another.

"But why?"

"It's part of my new strategy. Should something suddenly come up, as it so unfortunately did yesterday, you will step in as my cover—an assistant so to speak. In this way my faithful friend, Bones, I will be free to accomplish my goal of facing down the judges with my qualifications."

"Good idea."

"Thank you." Rick bowed. "Let's depart."

The ring of the telephone caught them on the porch step. Rick glanced at his watch. "No problem. We're still forty minutes to showdown. I allowed for minor interruptions."

"Hello?"

"Yes. Is Rick Masterson home?"

"This is he."

"Oh! Thank goodness! This is Clara, Rick. Where are you?" she demanded frantically.

"What do you mean?"

"I mean it's three-forty and you're still not here. I need to take a van load of kids home, and there's no one to cover for me."

Rick had forgotten to tell Clara or Heidi that he couldn't make it! He'd been so concerned over the interview that his work schedule had completely slipped his mind.

Fighting for control, he asked, "Is Heidi there?"

"No. She had to make a run to the bank, take two sick kids home and pick up some supplies. She's not due back for another hour yet."

Mind over matter. Subdue your environment, Rick said to himself.

There was a solution here, somewhere.

## The New Man

He glanced at his watch. "We'll be there in ten minutes." An idea began to form in his mind.

"But I don't know anything about kids!" B.R. protested, clinging to the dashboard as Rick made a corner turn onto Main.

"What's to know? You were a kid yourself not too long ago. People hang around kids all the time, remember?"

"Yeah, but Rick, I've had no experience—"

"No one's going to make trouble except Beany, and I'm pretty sure you're physically stronger than he is."

"How old is he?"

"Five."

"I don't know, Rick. It sounds bad."

"This is no time to turn coward, Bones." Rick pulled his truck into an alleyway and parked beside a row of aluminum garbage cans.

Clara was waiting for them at the door.

"Thank heavens you made it!" she said. Then she spotted B.R. "Who's this?"

"B.R., a friend of mine. I'm afraid he's going to have to watch the kids for about a half hour until Heidi gets back."

Clara's amiable expression vanished. "But, Rick, he's never been trained. Why can't you stay?"

"I have my interview for the scholarship at four-thirty."

"Wasn't that yesterday?"

"An emergency came up, and I missed it. Mrs. Bristol was kind enough to reschedule it for today."

"So you're the one." Clara said. "Isabel asked a few of us together for a special meeting last night to get the makeup interview approved. You passed by the skin of your teeth, Rick."

"I guessed as much. That's why it's so important that I'm prompt today."

"You should have called."

"I know. Those words are becoming my middle name. I'm really sorry."

Clara gave B.R. a skeptical glance. "All right, I don't see any other way, either. Show him around first, though. Don't let him go down without at least giving him a life jacket."

"Go down?" B.R. glanced at Rick.

"Will do. Thanks, Clara."

A few seconds later a loud crash of glass sounded from the toddlers' room. Clara moaned and started down the hall.

"We'll get it," Rick said, stopping her. "You go ahead."

Hesitantly she agreed, gesturing toward the room. "Remember about Beany. No spanking or bullying. Someone's coming by to pick him up early today, anyway. His grandparents are flying in and his family wants him with them at the airport."

"I give you my word, I'll do nothing more than murder him."

Clara forced an uneasy smile and herded her small flock of children toward the Humpty Dump-All van.

Rick turned and walked down the hall that reeked of melted crayons and tomato soup. A circle of kids had crowded around the giant jar of grape preserves. The contents slowly oozed into a bigger circle on the floor, and pieces of shattered glass glittered dangerously around them. Rick instantly checked their feet and, remarkably, they were all wearing shoes.

"Okay, everyone back," he commanded. "Who did this?"

They all spoke at once, but it was Sarah who clarified things by pointing her finger at Beany. He was sitting innocently at a table, profoundly absorbed with a coloring book.

"Beany did it. He sneaked into the wefwijwatoe and twied to eat the jaw of gwapes!"

Rick nodded. "All right, I want you guys to go to the bookshelves and find something interesting to look at until I get this cleaned up. If anyone moves from there, they'll have to skip snacks tomorrow. Do we all understand?"

"I'll get the pile of goo," B.R. offered. "You can inflict pain on that miniature vandal."

Rick shook his head. He knew B.R. had never seen a mess like this, let alone cleaned one up. There were tiny slivers of glass everywhere. If even one of them was overlooked and someone was cut, Rick would feel responsible. He glanced at his watch. There was still ten minutes left before he needed to leave, plenty of time to take care of the sticky mess before him.

"No, I'll get this. You take Beany to the corner and make sure he stays there until I'm done."

"But what about your clothes? Mrs. Bristol won't like those spots of grape jelly."

"Don't worry." Rick zigzagged across the room to Clara's cabinet drawer and shook out a pink smock-type apron. He swiftly ducked inside it and tied the bow around his waist.

B.R. made no cracks, but he couldn't help smiling at his friend's appearance.

Rick located a pail of soapy water, and the two young men busied themselves at their unlikely task.

The pile of preserves was not as unruly as Rick thought it would be. He corralled the slippery conglomeration onto a dustpan, wiped the purple splatters and hurriedly swept the area, completing the job with three minutes in his favor. It took a few seconds more to scan the floor for forgotten glass.

"Well, well, well. If we aren't the perfect mom," a voice sneered from the doorway.

Rick glanced up and spotted the tall body looming above the kids.

Wolf curled his lips into a sarcastic grin. "When did you become Mary Poppins, partner? Or is it, Mr. Mom?" He doubled over with exaggerated hilarity at his witticisms.

Beany heard him and sprang from the corner, ducking between B.R.'s legs to escape. "Hi, Wolf!"

he exclaimed excitedly. He jumped on a nearby tricycle in an attempt to show off for his older brother and peddled a figure eight around them. "Beep beep," he yelled so loudly they could scarcely hear anything else.

Wolf gave him a brief acknowledgement. "Hey, kid. Pretty speedy. It's time to go." Then turned his attention back to Rick.

Dissatisfied, Beany decided to display his talents further and zipped past him toward the hall.

"He's not allowed outside unescorted," Rick hastily informed Wolf, hoping he'd grab an arm to stop him.

"It's okay, he's with me now. Did any of these kids ever tell you that you make an ugly mother?"

"Lay off," B.R. interrupted.

"Thanks, Bones." Rick sighed. "Beany shouldn't be left unattended, Wolf. If you're not going to take charge of your kid brother, then I'll have to. A rule is a rule."

"Follow me, B.R. You can bring Beany inside again for checkout. The paper is on the desk. It's self-explanatory." He tapped his watch. "I've got to go."

Rick deposited the dustpan and pale of water in the sink and, untying the pink apron as he went, strode past Wolf. B.R. was like a shadow at his heel.

Beany was nowhere in the hall. "Wolf should never have let that kid out of his sight," Rick grumbled over his shoulder to B.R. "You never know what he's going to do. Even his mom leashes him before she allows him outside."

"It's only been a few seconds," B.R. said. "What could a kid do in a few seconds?"

"You'd be surprised," Rick said, stepping into the sunlight. His eyes searched the front yard.

Beany wasn't anywhere in sight.

Detecting the faint sound of "beep, beeps" again, Rick headed for the alleyway. He finally spotted Beany fast-peddling it down the center of the alley, his head purposefully over the handlebars.

"Beany get back here!" Rick commanded in a roar. The alley started off level, but turned into a steep slope several yards from the street. "Beany, freeze!" he bellowed again.

"Watch me!" the eager five-year-old yelled back. "Ebol Konebol! Superpower race-car driver!"

"I'm going to superpower your bottom!" Rick broke into a run after him. The tricycle started downhill and Beany yelped with surprise, lifting his legs outward as the pedals began spinning too rapidly for his feet to keep up.

Gathering all his strength for a fast sprint, Rick dashed after him. Beany had lost control of the bike, and if he didn't reach him in time, a crash was inevitable. Rick thought about commanding him to jump ship. In case he didn't reach him in time, a bounce and roll would be better than a high-impact collision. It was garbage day in Redona and dangerous rows of overflowing trash cans were at every lot.

Rick was quickly gaining ground. He had an excellent chance of catching him before anything happened. He made a split-second decision to let Beany stay on the bike and keep after him.

Beany's cries merged into a full-fledged scream. His bike started to curve toward the side of the alley, and Rick's heart leaped in panic. He pushed himself faster, his feet barely touching ground. When he was within two yards of the speeding tricycle, he lunged through the air to stop him.

He managed to turn the bike, but tripped in his landing and crashed into a stack of garbage cans, scattering them like pins in a bowling alley. For one brief instant he thought he and Beany had escaped injury. Then, the last container tumbled down.

It hit Rick solidly on his head. Beany's sobs, the clattering of the cans as they bounced down the hill, B.R.'s frantic shouts became dim traces of sound as he faded into a deep, unmindful darkness.

## Chapter Twelve

Tell them I'm not here!" Rick shouted, burying his head beneath his pillow to muffle the persistent rings.

"You better be careful of that bandage," B.R. warned from his perch beside the bed. "You don't want to go back to the emergency room to get your head wrapped again, do you?"

The house fell silent, indicating that someone had answered the phone downstairs, and Rick's face emerged from hiding. "Don't try to pretend that you're my friend," he snapped.

"Ah, come on, Rick. You're taking things too seriously."

"Hardly. As far as I'm concerned, I'm looking at a traitor."

"Not a traitor. An agent. Agent, agent, *agent!*"

Rick stared at B.R. with increasing irritation and disbelief. "Why did you do it, Bones?"

"Like I told you, I thought it would help. Here was a chance at free publicity. What better way to impress the judges than with a photo from the paper?" He grabbed the folded newspaper from the floor and turned it to the second page, attempting once again to plead his case. "I know the picture isn't the most flattering but try to see it from my point of view. The *Redona City Star* isn't exactly the *Chicago Tribune*. Still, it counts pretty high with the folks around here. That paper seemed the most opportune way to make a good situation out of a bad one. At least now the judges can see that you weren't lying. They'll know with black-and-white proof that you had a good reason for missing the second interview."

Rick exhaled into a moan as B.R. held the photo in front of his nose. It looked even worse than it had the first seven times he'd seen it. There he was sitting like a wino against a toppled garbage can. Trash was spread haphazardly around him. He was still wearing Clara's apron. Someone had positioned Beany on his lap for the snapshot. The subtitle read, "Redona Young Miss Homemaker Candidate Injured in Lifesaving Pursuit." There were approximately seven thousand subscriptions to the paper in Greenleaf County, meaning approximately seven thousand readers who, at this very moment, were probably laughing at Rick over their morning coffee.

The one saving point to the whole nightmare was the reporter's accompanying article. It was short and vague. It must have been too difficult making the story interesting with the facts the way they were, so it had been kept brief. Beany's tricycle was termed a "runaway vehicle," the alley was described as a "narrow, roller-coaster incline" and the garbage can full of automotive parts was labeled as a "flying object."

"Phone for you, Rick," Mr. Masterson announced, sticking his head inside the room. "I think I'm going to stop the calls after this one, though. The doctor said to make sure you rested that concussion."

Rick shoved the pillow beneath his head. "How can you rest a big bump?" he complained.

"You know what I mean," his father said. "B.R. will have to leave, too, I'm afraid."

"Don't worry about me, Mr. Masterson. I'm gone. You won't find this boy hanging around where he's not appreciated. Nope. You don't have to hit me with an encyclopedia. I know when I'm not wanted." He stood dramatically, but paused, hoping for some sign or word of forgiveness from his best friend. None was forthcoming. Placing the phone on Rick's bed, B.R. shrugged philosophically before leaving.

Rick took a deep breath and placed the receiver to his one exposed ear. "Hello?"

"Rick Masterson, how could you!"

"Joany?"

"You never said a word! Not one word!"

## The New Man

"I tried Joany, it's just that the time was never right."

"How sneaky and underhanded!"

"Really, I was going to explain everything."

"Sure you were. On the night of the banquet."

"Please, Joany, you have to believe me."

"And suppose you win? What will you do then?"

Rick hesitated, trying to think of the most honest answer he could give her. "Bank the check, I guess."

She burst into sobs.

"Listen, Joany, please," he begged. "There's nothing to cry about. I'm not going to win."

"How do you know?" Her voice trailed into a high-pitched whine. "Your credentials are as good as mine. Anyone can see that."

"Yes, but I missed the interview."

"You did?"

"And Mrs. Bristol won't allow me to make it up. I explained my situation to her, but she said I couldn't reschedule a second time. It's a rule."

"Oh." She cleared her throat. "I'm sorry to hear that, Rick."

"I think it was fate."

"I'm afraid we still won't be able to attend the banquet together. After all that's happened, I'm going to need some time to think about things."

"I understand."

"I hope your head gets better."

"Thank you."

"Goodbye, Rick."

"Goodbye, Joany."

It wasn't so bad, Rick thought to himself. He supposed the Day of the Apron and the Day of the Cats had prepared him for the Day of the Garbage Can. He'd expected the confrontation with Joany to leave him emotionally devastated, as though his heart had been stuffed in a blender and set on puree.

But, oddly, he felt relieved. He'd finally come clean with Joany, and thanks to his questionably devoted friend, B.R., the rest of the town, as well.

Besides, Joany's rejection was like adding a glass of water to the ocean. The fact that he'd lost the scholarship was so depressing that any new grief would simply be lost midst the old... he was already filled to capacity with his misery.

The phone rang again and he groaned.

Mr. Masterson stepped into the room. "I said I'd stop the calls, but I thought you might want to take this last one."

"Who is it?"

"Heidi."

He grabbed the receiver. "Hello?"

"You're famous, Rick! Have you seen the paper?"

"Please, don't remind me."

"How do you feel today? I tried to call earlier to see how you were, but the line was busy."

"I know. People have been phoning ever since the paper hit their driveways. I just talked to Joany a few minutes ago."

An awkward silence followed. When Heidi spoke again, she sounded unnaturally casual. "Did she call to see how you were?"

"Sort of." He'd never told Heidi that he'd failed to talk to Joany about his candidacy the past two Mondays. As far as she knew, Joany had been accepting of everything.

"Well, I'm going to ask, too. Do you feel any better today?"

"Sure. I've been able to eat a few things, and I haven't passed out yet."

"Good. Do you think you'll be doing well enough to go to the banquet next Friday?"

"How did you know about the banquet?"

"Clara told me. She's afraid that because of all that's happened, you won't want to go."

"She's right."

"Well, you're going to anyway, aren't you? All the finalists are supposed to attend."

"What makes you think I'm a finalist?"

"Those are the only ones who were interviewed." She giggled. "Didn't you know? If you received an appointment for an interview, that meant you were a finalist. They were supposed to tell you the good news after you met with the judges."

"That explains it. I never made it to the judges' part." He felt the gauze bandage that was wrapped tightly across one ear. It stretched all the way up his scalp to the crown of his head like a cotton swimming cap. He wanted to check one more time that the past few days had been real and not simply a bad dream. "I don't know, Heidi, going to the banquet is like pouring salt in a wound."

"But it's required. And Clara really wants you to come. She says your efforts have opened the doors of homemaking to men everywhere."

"Swell."

"Besides, I need a date."

Rick sat up in the bed much too quickly and felt his head swirl dizzily. "You do?"

"I sure do. Clara gave me a ticket, but I don't want to go alone."

"Don't you have a bunch of guys from your own town that would like to take you?"

"Of course. Thousands. But I prefer to go with you."

"I'll still have my bandage."

"That's okay."

"And I don't own a three-piece suit."

She laughed. "Neither do I. Anything else you'd like to confess?"

"No. At least I'm not aware of anything." The dizzy spell overtook him, and he fell helplessly back into his pillow.

"Rick? Rick, are you there?"

"Yeah. I think. I'll pick you up at six-thirty."

"Perhaps I should drive, Rick. It might be best considering the circumstances."

Thousands of white dots began twirling and spinning through the darkness behind Rick's closed eyes.

"Sounds good to me," he replied with great effort before drifting off.

Rick had tried to convince his parents to stay home the night of the Young Miss Homemaker awards banquet, but they had insisted on attending. They had told him that they were proud of Rick for making it so far with such stiff competition.

Heidi, too, was behaving as though she thought it was a privilege to be at Rick's side. She kept smiling up at him as they strolled arm in arm toward the auditorium. Rick's parents had gone ahead so as to be assured of seats. They'd asked Rick and Heidi to go along with them, but Rick explained that the night air felt good after being cooped up in his room so long.

It made a good excuse. In reality, he couldn't even feel the night air. Although most of the kids had accepted the news of his candidacy much better than he'd expected, he was still apprehensive about attending the banquet with everyone knowing the reason he was a Miss Homemaker finalist. If there had actually been a chance of him winning the scholarship, he wouldn't have felt so self-conscious.

He would have had two thousand dollars for consolation.

"Nervous?" Heidi asked.

He glanced at her, admiring how pretty she looked in the corduroy skirt he'd made. She'd bought a pink silk blouse to go with it to make the outfit dressy enough to wear to the banquet.

"Are you nervous, Rick?" she repeated.

"Do trees have leaves?"

She laughed, and his gloomy expression finally cracked into a grin.

"Thanks for coming tonight, Heidi," he said.

"Hey. I asked you, remember?"

"You asked me because you knew I wasn't going to go. If there's one thing I've learned about women in all this mess, it's that they're sly. You knew that if I were escorting you I'd agree to attend."

"You flatter me, Mr. Masterson," Heidi replied. "As if someone like you could ever be swayed by a lil' ole belle from Ridgemont."

"I'm suggesting more than that. I'd say I was wooed by a gorgeous babe who spreads jelly over peanut butter with more ease than any other woman I know."

"Well, you're right. I had my eye on you from the start."

Their conversation was interrupted by a crowd near the entrance of the auditorium. Rick stiffened as he spotted Joany standing to the side of the stream of people that was flowing slowly through the double doors. Wolf was leaning against the wall beside her, and by the frown on Joany's face, they appeared to be having trouble.

"Is that her?" Heidi asked, noticing Rick's sudden uneasiness.

"Yes, and that's Beany's older brother, Wolf, with her."

"I know. We've met."

"You have?"

"In the alley, after the paramedics arrived. You were still unconscious." Heidi withdrew her arm from Rick's as they moved closer to the arguing couple.

He was too absorbed with Joany to notice.

Rick was hoping she wouldn't notice him and the night would pass without either of them having to say a word to each other.

"Is that the best you could do?" Rick heard Joany ask Wolf. "It's wide enough to sleep on!"

"Sorry!" he snapped. "I don't got a lot of ties stacked in my closet. I had to borrow this one from my old man."

"Well, it looks right out of a clown act!" She drew her lips into a pout. "I don't mean to be snobbish, Wolf, but we're going to be in the spotlight. I think it's best you take it off."

He shrugged. "Ya got no problem there. This thing's giving my tonsils a hernia." He straightened from the wall and used both hands to tug the first loop out of his tie.

Rick quickly ducked his head, but not before Wolf had spied him.

"Hey, partner!" He called above the noise as if they were yards apart, instead of a few feet.

"Hello, Wolf."

Joany twisted around at the sound of his voice. Her mouth dropped open as she took in Heidi. She started to speak, but Wolf stepped in front of her.

"I want to thank you for rescuing Beany," he said to Rick. "That little runt could've really hurt himself." He glanced at the large square bandage that still covered the cut on Rick's temple. "How's the bump anyway?"

"Okay. I'm still here."

"No thanks to me." Wolf reached his hand forward to clasp Rick's. "Thanks again, partner. I mean that."

Rick could hardly maintain his cool. As far as he knew, this was Wolf's first attempt at courtesy. He didn't want to discourage him by passing out in shock.

"Forget it. How did Beany like his picture in the paper?"

"Are you kidding? We have copies taped all over the place. The refrigerator, the fishbowl, the toilet tank."

Heidi laughed at Beany's predictable reaction to fame.

Wolf's gaze became more than appreciative. "You look great, Heidi," he said.

Joany stepped forward and cleared her throat expectantly. Rick caught the hint. "I don't believe you two girls have met. Heidi, this is Joany; Joany, this is Heidi."

Heidi smiled warmly. Joany gave a sharp impersonal nod.

"It's nice you could come tonight," Joany said. "A last-minute date no doubt."

"It certainly was. I thought Rick would say no when I asked him." Heidi giggled, and glanced up, flirtatiously at her broad-shouldered companion.

There was a glint in Joany's eyes as she turned to Rick and rested her hand on his arm. "I forgot to tell you, Rick. We're having a celebration party at my house after the banquet. I was wondering if you could come."

It was at that precise moment that Rick realized how fortunate he was to have Heidi with him, instead of Joany. B.R. had been right. All these years he'd been so absorbed with trying to win Joany's affection that he couldn't see her for the girl she really was.

The ancient crush he'd suffered since grade school was beginning to fade fast. He found himself actually feeling sorry for Wolf. He would be spending his Friday with a girl who thought more of herself than anything else—except maybe her cats.

Rick would be passing the evening with Heidi.

Beautiful Heidi.

He put his arm around Heidi's shoulders, and she glanced at him, her eyes twinkling with surprise.

"I'm sorry, Joany, but we've made other plans. You and Wolf have a good time, though."

"Well, you are going to stay long enough to watch me—I mean, someone win, aren't you?" she demanded.

"Sure." He pulled Heidi along. "We'd better head inside now."

Heidi smiled at everyone. "It was nice seeing you again, Wolf. And it was nice meeting you, Joany," she said politely, as they turned toward the door.

"Is it because of your allergies that you refused her invitation?" Heidi whispered.

Rick found her small hand and squeezed it. "I think you know better than that," he said.

After introducing Heidi to a few of his friends, Rick accompanied her to the front of the room to get their plates. He endured several "homemaker" jokes about his candidacy as well as a few questionable compliments on the heroics that ended him in a pile of trash, with a big lump on his head.

He was glad he'd come anyway. He knew all of the Young Miss Homemaker finalists, and it was fun seeing them so excited and anxious about the upcoming announcement.

And then, there was Heidi. She seemed to make it all easier for him. Even when Mrs. Bristol found him in the crowd, he didn't feel nearly as uncomfortable speaking with her as he usually did. He supposed knowing the whole thing was over helped, too. There was nothing for him to be concerned about anymore. He could relax.

"It's an exciting night, isn't it, Mr. Masterson?" Mrs. Bristol observed.

"Yes, ma'am."

"Your suit looks nice. Much better than the last time I saw you," she added.

"Thank you."

## The New Man

She glanced at his plate. "That's my recipe for chicken pot pie. Did you think the crust looked all right?"

"As a matter of fact, I chose it specifically because it appeared to have been brushed with butter."

"Why that's exactly what I did, Mr. Masterson! I can see you're really going to be a star pupil in Home Economics II!"

"What?"

"You had better take your seat now. The first speaker is about to begin."

"Home Economics II?"

"Enjoy your dinner."

"It's not mandatory, is it?" His voice became louder as Mrs. Bristol started to disappear in the crowd.

"Rick," Heidi whispered, gently patting his shoulder. "She can't hear you anymore."

At the same moment the speaker tapped the microphone and asked that everyone take his seat. Mrs. Bristol was going to announce the winner.

The audience tensed. Rick was more relaxed than his fellow finalists. He had long since resigned himself to his defeat. Smiling to himself, he leaned back in his chair to listen to Mrs. Bristol's words.

"The average person seldom stops to think of the many skills required of a top homemaker," she began. "We take for granted the more basic ones of cooking, cleaning and sewing, but we are less apt to think of how helpful a solid knowledge of nutrition, mathematics and psychology, just to name a few, can be. Yet, even more important than the skills and academic qualifications is the attitude of the candidate. The Redona Society of American Homemakers was searching for one quality above all others."

She paused dramatically.

"Caring. We were looking for an individual who showed compassion and concern for others. I think that we have found that person.

"And now, without further ado, I'd like to introduce the winner to you. You may recognize our selection by the battle scars and the various bandages he has sported throughout the semester. And you may have heard about his, to say the least *unusual* exploits. But now I would like you to see him in a new light. Ladies and gentlemen, it gives me great pleasure to present the winner of the American Homemaker award—Mr. Rick Masterson!"

Rick was too dazed to feel his father's hearty slap on his back. His heart began to race like a jackhammer when he realized it was his name that had just echoed through the auditorium. The applause was overwhelming. Heidi hugged him and then urged him to his feet. With a flaming face, he started toward the stage.

It was nothing like his dreams.

For one thing, B.R. had never been in them. He was now, though, jumping for joy outside the auditorium's windows. Rick laughed at him, and he could tell by the way he kept dropping to the ground, hugging himself, he was laughing wildly back.

No girls fainted, but they were clapping. All of them wearing big happy smiles for him. And Mrs. Bristol, the least likely person he would ever have imagined, placed the prized envelope in his hand.

He looked out at the applauding crowd, a warm satisfaction swelling in his chest. Suddenly the future opened up before him. It would be a wonderful year, full of days with Heidi, afternoons at the nursery school, computer courses and...

*Home Economics II.*

# Take 4 Silhouette Romance novels FREE...

### and get more great Silhouette Romance novels

—for a 15-day FREE examination—
delivered to your door every month!

In addition to your 4 FREE Silhouette Romance® novels—yours to keep even if you never buy a single additional book—you'll have the opportunity to preview 6 new books as soon as they are published.

Examine them in your home for 15 days FREE. When you decide to keep them, pay just $1.95 each, *with no shipping, handling, or other charges of any kind!*

Each month, you'll meet lively young heroines and share in their escapades, trials and triumphs... virile men you'll find as attractive and irresistible as the heroines do...and a colorful cast of supporting characters you'll feel you've always known.

Delivered right to your door will be heart-felt romance novels by the finest authors in the field, including Diana Palmer, Brittany Young, Rita Rainville, and many others.

You will also get absolutely FREE, a copy of the Silhouette Books Newsletter with every shipment. Each lively issue is filled with news about upcoming books, interviews with your favorite authors, even their favorite recipes.

When you take advantage of this offer, you'll be sure not to miss a single one of the wonderful reading adventures only Silhouette Romance novels can provide.

To get your 4 FREE books, fill out and return the coupon today!

*This offer not available in Canada.*

## Silhouette Romance®

Silhouette Books, 120 Brighton Rd., P.O. Box 5084, Clifton, NJ 07015-5084

---

**Clip and mail to: Silhouette Books,
120 Brighton Road, P.O. Box 5084,
Clifton, NJ 07015-5084**

**YES.** Please send me 4 Silhouette Romance novels FREE. Unless you hear from me after I receive them, send me six new Silhouette Romance novels to preview each month as soon as they are published. I understand you will bill me just $1.95 each (a total of $11.70) with no shipping, handling, or other charges of any kind. There is no minimum number of books that I must buy, and I can cancel at any time. The first 4 books are mine to keep.

**BR28L6**

| Name | (please print) | |
|---|---|---|
| Address | | Apt. # |
| City | State | Zip |

Terms and prices subject to change. Not available in Canada.
SILHOUETTE ROMANCE is a service mark and registered trademark.
SilR-SUB-2

# First Love from Silhouette

## DON'T MISS THESE FOUR TITLES—AVAILABLE THIS MONTH...

---

### ORINOCO ADVENTURE  Elaine Harper
**A Blossom Valley Romantic Adventure!**
When Juanita heard charismatic Tom Goulding describe the Community Health program, she was determined to join the group—even if it meant traveling to the wilds of Venezuela.

### VIDEO FEVER
**Kathleen Garvey**
Who would have guessed that when arch enemies Nell and Daniel were forced to collaborate on a video project they would zoom in and focus on their very personal script?

### THE NEW MAN
**Carrie Lewis**
In spite of himself, when Rick Masterson decided to compete for the Young Miss Homemaker Award, he became the model for the liberated man. Heidi was not surprised. She had known the real Rick all along.

### WRITE ON!
**Dorothy Francis**
Vonnie was on the move again! The heroine of *Special Girl* and *Bid for Romance* had attendant problems to solve: just who was sending her those threatening notes, and why?

# WATCH FOR THESE TITLES FROM FIRST LOVE COMING NEXT MONTH

## SOMEONE ELSE Becky Stuart
### A Kellogg and Carey Story
When Carey's New York neighbor vanished overnight, Kellogg and Theodore joined in the search. This led them to some unexpected conclusions.

## ADRIENNE AND THE BLOB
### Judith Enderle
What in the world was Adrienne going to do about the blob? Only Tuck thought he knew, and he wasn't about to tell.

## BLACKBIRD KEEP
### Candice Ransom
Holly knew at once that she never should have agreed to visit her uncle. His house was too spooky and its inhabitants even weirder. Would Kyle help her to unravel the mystery, or was he working against her?

## DAUGHTER OF THE MOON
### Lynn Carlock
From childhood, Mauveen had known that somehow she was "different." Should she listen to the ancient ancestral voices, or should she follow the promptings of her newly awakened heart?

*First Love from Silhouette*

# Take 4 First Love from Silhouette novels FREE

That's right. When you take advantage of this special offer, you not only get 4 FREE First Love from Silhouette® novels, you also get the chance to preview 4 brand-new titles—delivered to your door every month—as soon as they are published.

A. a member of the First Love from Silhouette Book Club you'll receive stories about girls...and guys...you've known or would like to have as friends. These touching stories are yours for just $1.95 each, with no shipping, handling or other charges of any kind!

As an added bonus, you'll also get the First Love from Silhouette Newsletter FREE with every shipment. Each issue is filled with news about upcoming books and interviews with your favorite authors.

You can cancel your membership in the Club at any time, and the first 4 books are yours to keep.

Simply fill out and return the coupon today!

*This offer not available in Canada.*

## *First Love from Silhouette®*

**Silhouette Books, 120 Brighton Rd., P.O. Box 5084, Clifton, NJ 07015-5084**

---

**Clip and mail to: Silhouette Books,
120 Brighton Road, P.O. Box 5084, Clifton, NJ 07015-5084**

YES. Please send me 4 First Love from Silhouette novels FREE. Unless you hear from me after I receive them, send me four new First Love from Silhouette novels to preview each month as soon as they are published. I understand you will bill me $1.95 each (a total of $7.80) with no shipping, handling, or other charges of any kind. There is no minimum number of books that I must buy and I can cancel at any time. The first 4 books are mine to keep.   **BF18S6**

Name _____ (please print) _____

Address _____ Apt. # _____

City _____ State _____ Zip _____

Terms and prices subject to change. Not available in Canada.
FIRST LOVE FROM SILHOUETTE is a service mark and registered trademark. FL-SUB-1